The Colonial Countess

The Colonial Countess

ROBIN BELL

Library of Congress Control Number:		2017902166
ISBN:	Hardcover	978-1-5245-2257-5
	Softcover	978-1-5245-2256-8
	eBook	978-1-5245-2255-1

Print information available on the last page.

Rev. date: 02/14/2017

To order additional copies of this book, contact:
Xlibris
1-800-455-039
www.Xlibris.com.au
Orders@Xlibris.com.au
754850

CHAPTER 1

Victoria, Australia
Late December, 1885

Despite the need to get home for the evening milking, seventeen-year-old Mary Evans couldn't resist pausing at the top of the hill to gaze at the view she loved so dearly. The rolling hills, bathed in sunlight and the flats with dairy and beef cattle grazing in the paddocks stretching down to the sea sparkling on the horizon. After a couple of minutes, she sighed and turned her horse, knowing she had a busy afternoon and evening ahead of her, and before she could relax for a short time after dinner before going to bed.

As Trixie cantered slowly along the drive to the farmyard, Mary thought about the letter in her pocket. They rarely received letters these days, let alone ones from overseas. Stratford, Synbeck & Lyons, Solicitors, sounded very formal and she wondered why they would be writing to her mother from England.

After leaving the groceries and mail in the kitchen and checking that her mother was comfortable on couch beside the fire in the living room, Mary went out to the dairy to assist her stepbrother Graham milk the small herd of cows they still owned following their father's tragic death fighting a bushfire two years ago.

They chatted as they milked, then while Graham shut the cows in their paddock, Mary fed the chooks and locked them in their shed, shut the pigs in their sty, and chained the dogs to their kennels before heading to the kitchen for dinner.

Aunt Clara, their father's sister, lived on the farm with them, doing most of the housework and cooking, while Mary and Graham did the farm work. She also nursed Patricia, Mary's mother, who was virtually bedridden these days following a severe bout of influenza two months ago, which had left her with a severe cough and muscle weakness.

Following dinner, Patricia read the Solicitor's letter, then asked to be taken straight to bed and for Mary to bring her a large yellow envelope from a drawer in her desk. Once settled in bed, Patricia told Mary that the letter from England was from her mother's solicitor, asking her to return to England as soon as possible. According to the letter, Patricia's brother David had been killed in a riding accident and her mother was desperate to see her long lost daughter again.

Mary was astounded to hear this news, as until this moment she had no idea she had a grandmother, and until recently, an uncle in England. Her mother had always been very reticent to talk about her life before arriving in Australia and meeting her husband Tom, a widower with a two year-old son, Graham.

Imagine Mary's shock when she saw that the Solicitor addressed her mother as Lady Patricia! However, when Mary questioned her about this, Patricia became quite agitated and breathless.

Later, she told Mary that she would need to go to see her Grandmother in her stead, as she would not be able to undertake a three-month sailing voyage in her state of health. The contents of the yellow envelope, plus a key taped to the desk drawer were to be taken to Mr Lyons, the solicitor, at his office in Lewes in southern England.

Following a longer than usual bout of coughing, Patricia told Mary she would explain all about her family, but would like a cup of tea first. Much to Mary's horror, when she entered the bedroom a few minutes later, she found her mother lying motionless on the bed, eyes staring sightlessly at the ceiling.

Three days later, on the first day of the New Year, Patricia was laid to rest beside her beloved Tom in the local cemetery. Mary was the sole beneficiary of Patricia's will, which consisted mainly of a few pieces of jewellery and a small amount of money. The farm was now Graham's, so Mary was at a bit of a loss as to what the future might hold for her.

As the days passed, Mary began to think more about the mystery of her mother's family in England and she reread the Solicitor's letter. He said a Solicitor in Melbourne had been instructed to arrange and pay for Patricia's passage to England, and this led Mary to wonder if those instructions would now apply to her if she decided to go to England. She discussed the pros and cons with Graham and Aunt Clara, and it was decided that Mary should at least take the train to Melbourne and speak to the Solicitor Mr Mee.

So, a fortnight following Patricia's death, and two days after her eighteenth birthday, Mary arrived at Flinders Street Station on a hot January morning, feeling stiff and sore after her first time travelling in a train, sitting on a hard wooden seat for the three-hour journey.

After a refreshing cup of tea at the station, she hired a cab to the Solicitor's address in King Street. Walking up the stairs to the office on the third floor, Mary began to have serious doubts about what she was about to do, but then decided she was being pathetic. She knocked on the door with Mr Mee's name on it, and entered before she could change her mind.

A young lady at the desk looked up from her typewriter and smiled, asking how she could be of assistance. Mary handed her the letter and asked if she could please see Mr Mee. The letter was taken through to another office and almost immediately, a young man appeared and asked Mary to be seated at the desk in the inner office.

He introduced himself as Charles Mee, and asked Mary why she wished to see him in relation to the letter. Mary explained about her mother's wish for her to go to England in her stead and her sudden death not long afterwards. She also spoke of her total lack of knowledge of her mother's early life and family in England, and her shock at seeing the reference to her mother as Lady Patricia.

Mary asked if the reference to arranging and paying for passage to England could be transferred to herself, and on seeing a copy of her mother's will, Mr Mee said he could see no reason why not.

Suddenly, Mary found herself having to think seriously about what a trip to England would entail. Mr Mee said he would look into booking passage on the next steam ship bound for England, and suggested Mary stay at the Windsor Hotel until arrangements could be made.

He quickly added that all expenses would be covered, much to Mary's relief, as she had very little money left following her journey to Melbourne. He then asked the young lady at the front desk to accompany Mary to the hotel and book a suite for her. As they were saying goodbye, he handed Mary a heavy leather purse and instructed her to leave it in the hotel safe after removing money for ongoing expenses.

The next three days were a blur of totally new experiences for Mary. She had never seen such splendour as the foyer of the hotel, the rooms of her suite that would have housed a family at home, and the dining room and food were beyond her belief!

When she tentatively asked how she was to pay for all this luxury, she was told it was all taken care of. By whom, she wondered and why.

The crowds on the streets and the shop windows fascinated Mary, though she was careful not to wander too far on her own. Mr Mee called to see her just after lunch on the third day, to inform her she was booked on a ship sailing for England in two days' time.

He introduced her to his Aunt Felicity who would also be travelling to England on the same ship and was seeking a female companion for the trip. Like Mary, she had never travelled abroad and was rather apprehensive of being on her own. Throughout the afternoon, they chatted about all sorts of things and found themselves to be quite comfortable in each other's company.

Felicity had a list of clothing and other things they would need for the three-month journey, so the next day, they went shopping for all that was required. Felicity had been left very comfortably well off by her deceased husband, and Mary had been assured that her family in England would pay all costs.

Mary, however, was still very careful not to go overboard with her spending, never having been in the habit in the past of wasting money on things she really didn't need.

CHAPTER 2

The next day, all their luggage was taken to the ship and just before they too were taken to board the ship, Mary posted a long letter to Graham and Aunt Clara, explaining that she was about to sail for England and apologising for not getting back to say goodbye in person.

The ship towered above them as they stood on the dock, and seemed just as huge when they climbed the gangplank and stood on the deck, waiting to be taken to their cabins. Mary was delighted but rather stunned to find she had a first class cabin all to herself, while Felicity was in a similar cabin a little further down the passageway.

They both went out onto the deck to watch as the ship sailed down the bay and out through the Heads to Bass Strait, each of them wondering if they would ever return.

Thankfully, both Mary and Felicity were good sailors, and were two of the few passengers who regularly met in the dining room for meals during the first three days of the journey, when the weather was extremely windy and the huge waves seemed to toss the large ship around like a cork.

After their first stop at Albany on the southern tip of West Australia, the ship headed north into the Indian Ocean en route to the next stop at Galle, a port on the island of Ceylon. Apart from a couple of rather violent storms, the trip was uneventful. Both women enjoyed the journey immensely, filling their time with the many activities on the ship, reading books from the ship's library or just chatting as they wandered on the deck, or sat in the passengers' lounge.

By now, the weather had become quite hot as they crossed the equator, and neither lady ignored the stewardess's suggestion to divest themselves of as much of their heavy under garments as possible, and to wear cotton dresses if they had them.

Both Felicity and Mary enjoyed getting off the ship at Galle, keen to stretch their legs and see some of the sites near the port, before the ship headed to Suez, to begin the much anticipated journey through the Suez Canal to Port Said on the Mediterranean Sea. The canal was quite narrow, the banks seemingly quite close to the sides of the big steam ship as it slowly made its way towards Port Said. There were a couple of lakes where ships could pass so their progress was unimpeded.

The Mediterranean Sea was calm and the weather fine for most of the journey to Marseille, the French port where some of the passengers disembarked before the final leg through the Straits of Gibraltar, into the Atlantic Ocean, then the English Channel and finally, early one early April morning, the ship sailed up the River Thames and berthed at the Royal Albert Dock, London. The journey had taken two and a half months, the Suez Canal cutting the time by weeks.

While Mary and Felicity were a little sad that they were to go their separate ways when they docked, they were also relieved to be at the end of their sea voyage and were looking forward to having solid ground under their feet once again. Felicity left her sister's address with Mary, who promised she would write once she found out where she was going.

CHAPTER 3

England
Mid-April, 1886

Before she left the ship, the purser told Mary an associate of Mr Lyons, the Solicitor who had written the letter to her mother, would meet her on the dock and collect her luggage for her. She was introduced to Ben when she stepped off the gangplank. He cheerfully greeted her in an accent she found hard to understand, then showed her into a waiting hansom cab before proceeding to instruct porters to gather Mary's luggage and stow it in the second cab.

As they left the dock, Ben told Mary they were going to Paddington Station where they would catch the afternoon train to Lewes—a town in Sussex, about sixty five miles south of London—and should arrive there late in the afternoon.

After lunch at Paddington Station, Mary was taken to the front of the train and found herself in a well-appointed carriage with padded leather seats—a far cry from the hard wooden seat she sat on when travelling to Melbourne.

Mary was apprehensive, yet also excited about her unknown future as she travelled through countryside so different to what she was accustomed to. The trees were so different in shape and colour to the gum trees she was so fond of at home.

When the train arrived at Lewes later in the afternoon, Ben escorted Mary to the White Hart Hotel, where a middle-aged gentleman—dressed in a black suit and holding a bowler hat—met them in the foyer.

When Ben introduced Mary to Mr Lyons, the Solicitor, he stared at her with a puzzled frown before saying how pleased he was to meet her.

A little shaken by his distant reception, Mary began to seriously wonder what had possessed her to travel to the other side of the world with no knowledge of what awaited her. However, after his initial surprise in seeing her—he was after all expecting her mother she supposed—Mr Lyons booked her a room at the hotel.

Over a much-needed cup of tea in the hotel dining room, he enquired about her trip and her first impressions of England that she had seen on the train journey. She told him the countryside was much different from what she was used to in Australia.

Mr Lyons had spent a lot time watching Mary as she spoke, then excused himself for his rudeness saying how much she looked like her mother when he had last seen her nearly twenty years ago. He then asked Mary about her mother's life in Australia, her marriage, children, the farm, and finally her death.

Mary once again found herself telling the story of the arrival of his letter and the subsequent events leading to her arrival in Lewes. She also informed him of her lack of knowledge of her mother's background and her anxiety regarding the money being spent on her behalf, without knowing why or how she was to pay it back.

As Mary began to show signs of exhaustion after her travels, Mr Lyons suggested she retire to her room for a rest, while he read through the contents of the sealed yellow envelope that her mother had given to her. He also took the key she wore on a chain around her neck, saying it was for a security box at the bank.

That evening, Mr Lyons, his wife, and Mary had dinner at the hotel. Mrs Lyons was very keen to hear about Mary's life in Australia and was amazed to hear of the native animals Mary spoke about, especially the kangaroos. Before they parted at the end of the meal, arrangements were made for Mary to meet Mr Lyons at his office across the road at 9 a.m. the next morning, when he said he would explain everything.

CHAPTER 4

The next morning, Mary was ushered into Mr Lyon's office and seated in one of the two lounge chairs near a glowing coal fire. She was told to prepare herself for some rather startling information that might take some time to adjust to.

Her maternal Grandmother, Lady Emma Everton, was a Countess who had apparently died a week before her daughter Patricia. Meaning, Patricia—inheriting the hereditary title—was unknowingly a Countess for just a week and on her death, the title passed to Mary.

On saying this, Mr Lyons stood up in front of Mary, bowed and told her it gave him great pleasure to be the first person to greet her with her full title—Lady Mary Emma Evans, Countess of Longmire and Oakdale.

Mary sat stunned for a moment, and then started to laugh, much to Mr Lyons' chagrin. It took a while for her to realise he was being very serious and that maybe she should listen to the full story.

As the elder of two children, Lady Patricia was the heir to her mother's heraldic title, a fact bitterly resented by her younger brother David. He tormented his sister throughout their childhood and into their teenage years whenever he was home from boarding school, until the day Lady Patricia suddenly disappeared, just a month after her father's death.

David said she had slipped and fallen into the river and had been swept away; but they never found any trace of her body or her clothing, and there was always some doubt but no proof of her death. Her mother—the Countess—was grief stricken, but was finally forced to concede that in Patricia's absence, David would become her heir.

David was the total antithesis to Lady Patricia. While Patricia was of a sunny disposition—always helping others and wonderful with children and animals—David was surly and cruel to people and animals alike.

Although the Countess was forced to name David as her heir, she didn't trust him, so had a codicil added to her will that should she die by accident or misadventure, David would not have the title nor the fortune and lands that went with it.

Consequently, he spent most of his time living in the family residence in London, spending his allowance as quickly as he received it, gambling and drinking to excess, and growing more bitter and unpleasant as the years passed.

Unfortunately for David, lack of concern for his horse, combined with a bad hangover clouding his judgement on a frosty morning, led to him parting company with his horse when he tried to make it jump a large hedge. He was found barely alive with a broken back and taken to the local doctor's surgery where he died later that afternoon.

It appeared he made a deathbed confession to the doctor that he had arranged and paid for his sister to be kidnapped, drugged, and put on a ship sailing to Melbourne, Australia. The couple paid to accompany Patricia, virtually as her gaolers, were told she was a thief and escapee from the asylum and was to be kept locked in a cabin for the whole trip.

As soon as the Countess was informed of this confession, she sent people to Australia to search for any information about her beloved daughter. As Patricia had very similar features to her mother, a sketch of the Countess was sent with the private detectives.

Finally, after nine months, word had arrived of a woman married to a Victorian farmer who may be the lady being sort. A detective in Melbourne thought he had spoken to Mary's mother when he called at the farm to ask for instructions to the next town.

This led to the letter that Patricia received just prior to her death, being sent. Unfortunately, letters to and from the colony took over three months to arrive so it was a further seven months before the letter was delivered. Unbeknown to Patricia, her mother had caught a chill and died just a week before her daughter. The wording of Patricia's will, which hadn't made much sense to Mary at the time, ascertained Mary's ascension to the title and all it pertained.

Poor Mary was totally confused and unsure what all this meant to her, so Mr Lyons told her he would have some tea and cake sent in, and would give her time to digest the information she had been given so far, before telling her more about her new situation.

About half an hour later, Mary asked Mr Lyons to explain how this astounding news would affect her future. He started by saying she was now a Peer of the Realm, an extremely rich young lady, owner of thousands of acres of land, with stewardship over many thousands more, plus owner of numerous businesses in England and overseas.

The family residence Longmire Hall, was about six miles from Lewes, with three farms, and Longmire village within the vast Longmire Estate. Another large acreage, Oakdale Estate, was up north in Yorkshire and there was also the family residence in London.

Head reeling, Mary agreed to go out to lunch, and then to visit the bank to have the accounts changed to her name. However, when she was asked if she wished to go to her new residence that afternoon, she said she would prefer to spend the night at the hotel to try to get her head around all this incredible information.

CHAPTER 5

The next morning, Mary was astounded when people addressed her as My Lady—or as it sounded m'lady—the women curtseying and men bowing their heads to her as she made her way to the breakfast room for breakfast with Mr Lyons and Ben.

Amused at Mary's confusion, Ben explained that as a Countess, people speaking to her would refer to her as My Lady—not Mary as she was used to—and she would be referred to as Lady Mary when being spoken about. Her full title would be used when she was introduced to new acquaintances, or at formal occasions.

Soon afterwards, Mary and Mr Lyons left Lewes in a hansom cab, Mr Lyons patiently explaining what Mary was likely to be confronted with when they arrived at the Longmire Estate. A message had been sent ahead to advise the household of her potential arrival that morning.

As Mary was trying to take all this in, she was also observing the countryside they were travelling through. So different to what she was used to in Australia, yet quite appealing in a way she couldn't quite fathom. At first, this confused Mary; then she remembered that she was now on the other side of the world, and although it was summer when she left Melbourne in January, it was now spring in England.

About half an hour later, the cab passed through two imposing wrought iron gates opened by an elderly gateman who doffed his hat and bowed at the waist as they passed. The wide driveway passed through a dense woodland of trees Mary had never seen before, many just starting to burst into leaf. The woodland changed to open parkland with some black faced sheep grazing a little way from the driveway.

Mary had lived her whole life in a modest single storey wooden farmhouse in Australia, and so was totally unprepared for her first sight of her new home—Longmire Hall—as the cab rounded a curve. Before her, at the end of the driveway, stood an imposing white multi-storey building with elegant steps leading up to an impressive portico and stout wooden front door. Windows seemed to cover the whole of the building's façade, with numerous dormer attic windows under a high-pitched roof with countless chimneys. Set on a slight slope of immaculate lawn with what looked like a small lake to the side, the whole scene seemed like a fairy tale to Mary.

As the cab stopped at the marble steps, a man appeared to hold the horse's head, to allow Mr Lyons help Mary down from the cab. The front door opened and a tall, thin lady dressed in a long black dress appeared and waited at the top as they ascended the six steps.

Mr Lyons introduced Mary to Mrs Howard, the Housekeeper, who led them through the front door into a huge, high ceilinged hallway with a black-and-white tiled floor. There was a wide, beautifully carved staircase, dividing to lead to landings on the left and right of the hall, with a large, framed landscape painting adorning the wall at the top of the stairs.

Mary was guided through a door into a sitting room with a fire blazing in the large ornate fireplace, and a magnificent view through large French doors of manicured green lawns leading down to the lake.

Mr Lyons asked Mrs Howard to bring the indoor staff to the sitting room in five minutes. Mary was beginning to feel very intimidated by her situation, but was assured all would be well, and for her just to be polite and formal with the staff.

Mrs Howard introduced her to Mrs Smith, the cook; Polly the parlour maid, and Jane the kitchen maid; all of whom curtsied and said, 'good morning, my lady' in unison. She was told there was also the groom, stable hand, gardener and his assistant, to whom she would be introduced later. There was also apparently an Estate manager who was at the time away from the Estate.

Following lunch with just Mr Lyons and herself sitting at a dining table large enough to seat twenty four, Mr Lyons had to leave to go back to his office in Lewes, assuring Mary he would keep in touch. He suggested Mary be shown some of the house to which Mrs Howard begrudgingly said she would make time to do so.

Half an hour later, Mary was relieved to retire to her room, staggered at the size and number of rooms she had been shown, and she had yet to see many of the bedrooms, the nursery wing, and the servants' rooms in the attics, plus two more wings, but more so to get away from Mrs Howard's barely disguised contempt and ill feeling towards her.

Her own bedroom on the first floor was immense, seeming to Mary to be about half the size of their house at home. There was a large four-poster bed with curtains tied back; a charming fireplace with a glowing coal fire; two lounge chairs and window seats under the two large windows that looked out to the lake. There was also a dressing room and a bathroom with the largest bath she had ever seen.

In fact, everything in the Hall appeared to be of huge proportions. Next to the bathroom was a smaller bedroom (still larger than her bedroom at home) that Mary assumed had been used by her grandmother's maid.

Not sure how to spend the rest of the afternoon, Mary went back down to the sitting room, taking with her a book from her luggage that had been taken to her room and unpacked while she was at lunch. She wasn't sure she liked the idea of someone else going through her personal things, but decided not to say anything until she had a better understanding of what was expected of her, and what she could or should and shouldn't do. So far, everything seemed to be run extremely formally.

Dinner that night was a lonely affair for Mary, sitting at the head of the long empty dining table. Though delicious, there was far too much food for Mary to eat—she just hoped it wouldn't be wasted. Polly stood silently near the table, serving the various courses and removing dishes as Mary finished the soup, the main course, and then dessert. Not sure should she speak to Polly, Mary stayed silent other than to thank her for serving her meal.

Again, at a loss as to what should be done when the meal was completed, Mary excused herself and went up to her bedroom. As she entered the room, she felt so miserable. The homesickness she had managed to control throughout most of her journey swept over her and she lay on the bed and sobbed into her pillow.

Sometime later, she wasn't sure how long, she heard a gentle tap on the door and Polly anxiously asked was she alright and could she come in. Assuring Polly she was fine—just exhausted from travelling—Mary asked her who had unpacked her luggage. Polly replied she had, as that was part of her job and hoped she had put everything in the right place.

She also said she would be looking after Lady Mary's rooms and would be at her service should she require anything, pointing to the bell pull near the fireplace. She told Mary she would normally come up to the bedroom after dinner to close the curtains, turn down the bed, and if it was cold, warm the sheets with a bed warmer before Mary came up to bed.

Encouraged by this short conversation with Polly, Mary enquired what time should she go down for breakfast in the morning, to which Polly replied that breakfast would be served at whatever time she requested. Not quite sure what time to ask for, she asked Polly what time the servants usually started work in the kitchen each morning.

Polly told her that Jane went down to the kitchen at 6.00 each morning to fire up the range and put the kettle on, while Polly followed soon after to set the fires in the breakfast and sitting rooms. Mrs Smith would be in the kitchen by 6.30 a.m. when they would all have a cup of tea before breakfast was prepared for the indoor and outdoor staff. However, now the new Countess was in residence, they were awaiting her directions as to what their morning schedule would be.

Taking a deep breath before issuing her first direct instruction to a servant, Mary told Polly she would like to have her breakfast at 7.30 the next morning. Polly told her she would let Mrs Smith know, then asked if Mary would like a cup of tea brought to her room before she dressed.

CHAPTER 6

Mary was roused the next morning by Polly's gentle tap on her door. She entered carrying a tray bearing a china teapot, milk jug and cup and saucer—all with the same delicate floral pattern—a red rose in a vase, and a small white card with a hand written message 'Welcome Lady Mary'. As she opened the curtains, Polly told Mary that the servants were pleased to have a mistress in the house again, as the past four months since her Grandmother's death had been hard as nobody knew what was to happen.

Mary drank her tea, then dressed in a skirt, blouse and jacket.—She wasn't at all interested in the ladies' fashions she'd seen in London and Lewes but supposed she would have to have some for formal occasions. She carefully tucked the card in her bag then went downstairs, hoping she could remember where the breakfast room was.

Mrs Howard was waiting for her at the bottom of the stairs, and after a brief greeting, led Mary to the breakfast room. At the doorway, she brusquely told Mary she should speak to her first before talking to the servants as she, Mrs Howard, was the only one to instruct them.

Stung by this rebuke, Mary poured herself a cup of coffee from the sideboard laden with steaming dishes, and sat beside the fire wondering how she was going to deal with this situation. Mary had the feeling Mrs Howard didn't approve of her being there, why, she wasn't sure.

Wherever Mary went in the house after breakfast, the housekeeper seemed to be present and always intervened if Mary tried to speak to any of the servants. It appeared Mrs Howard was a hard task master to the indoor servants, and Mary was horrified at her constant berating of them for what seemed very trivial issues.

During the next few days, Mary was extremely miserable, feeling very alone and at a total loss as to what she could or couldn't do in the house. Mrs Howard made no effort to help, seeming to take great delight in her growing misery. Neither Polly, Jane, nor Mrs Smith were allowed to speak to Mary, and Mrs Howard demanded they stand with their heads bowed if Mary was nearby, and to only respond with either 'yes' or 'no, m'lady' if Mary spoke to them.

At first, Polly tried to speak to Mary when alone with her in her bedroom but the poor girl was severely reprimanded by the housekeeper following her trips to Mary's room and was forced to enter and leave with the barest acknowledgment to Mary. Both thought Mrs Howard must listen at the keyhole while they were in the bedroom.

As a naturally active, independent young lady used to working hard from dawn to dusk, there was no way she could live the sedentary, empty life it appeared she was destined to endure at Longmire Hall, thanks to the title of 'Countess' that had so suddenly descended upon her.

CHAPTER 7

Mary's only release during the boring, lonely days of her first week at the Longmire Estate was to go for walks in the parkland, or to visit the stables where Mrs Howard had minimal influence.

A keen rider and horse lover, Mary took great delight in meeting the half dozen horses in the paddock—or as she was told, the field beside the stables. The four black horses were the coach horses, while the two bays, Rusty and Tiger, were usually used to pull the cart and buggy, though they had been broken to ride.

When asked why there were no riding horses, Robert, the groom, explained that they had all been sold following Mr David's death. Mary decided she would need to buy herself a new horse and asked for Robert's advice.

Robert was thrilled to discover the new mistress was interested in the horses and was happy to discuss them with her. Mrs Howard on the other hand, told Mary it was not correct for a person of her status to visit the stables alone, and certainly not to talk to the groom. However, despite Mrs Howard's orders not to do so, Robert encouraged Mary to talk about her life in Australia during her visits to the stables.

During their discussions, Robert soon began to realise that their new Countess, although young and struggling with the peculiarity of her new life, was a lady with a mind of her own and a strong belief in right and wrong. Quite the opposite of the uneducated, unskilled peasant from the colonies that Mrs Howard was suggesting Mary must be, during the staff meals in the kitchen. She was sure she wouldn't last a fortnight at Longmire. Robert didn't agree but made no comment.

After breakfast on her first Sunday at Longmire Hall, Robert drove Mary to the Longmire village church a mile away, while the rest of the servants walked. Several people were waiting outside the church, no doubt to see the new Countess, but no one moved until the Vicar introduced himself and led Mary to the family pew at the front of the church, where Mary sat throughout the service in solitary isolation.

When everyone followed Mary and the Vicar outside, a couple of ladies introduced themselves and told Mary they remembered Lady Patricia well and were very sorry to hear of her sudden death. However, everyone else quickly left the church yard, but not before Mary heard words like 'upstart, too young, and won't last,' muttered from a group talking with Mrs Howard.

Back at the Hall, Mary went into the sitting room to await lunch and sat staring into the fire wondering what in the world she should do. Suddenly, she felt as though her mother was in the room with her, telling her she was now the mistress in her own home and that Mrs Howard was obliged to carry out her wishes.

Mary knew there was a servant's hierarchy, according to position and length of tenure, but she was, after all, their employer and had ultimate authority—even over Mrs Howard! During lunch, Mary decided that if she was to assert her authority, it was best not to procrastinate, so, as she left the dining room she asked Polly to tell Mrs Howard she wished to see her immediately in the sitting room.

After waiting five minutes, Mary went to the kitchen to find Mrs Howard sitting at the table with a glass of wine in her hand, telling the other servants the young upstart could wait and she would go when she was ready. Furious at such blatant insubordination, Mary removed the glass from Mrs Howard's hand, placed it on the table and ordered the housekeeper to go to the sitting room straight away.

Before she too left the kitchen, Mary asked Polly if she had used the word 'immediately' when she passed on the message. She replied that she had, but Mrs Howard had just laughed and said she could wait.

When Mary entered the sitting room, she walked past Mrs Howard, who was standing in the middle of the room, and stood looking out at the lake before she turned slowly to face the housekeeper. For once, Mrs Howard appeared to realise she had overstepped the mark and looked a little apprehensive as Mary stared at her.

In a quiet, measured voice, Mary told Mrs Howard she wasn't prepared to put up with the housekeeper's discourteous behaviour towards her, and that unless she accepted the fact that Mary was her employer and was to be given due respect at all times, her employment would be terminated.

Mrs Howard was speechless, staring at Mary as though she couldn't believe what she was hearing. Without saying a word, she turned and stormed out of the room, slamming the door behind her.

Mary decided to give her some time to calm down and went out through the French windows into the garden. She had only been out there for a short while when she heard a scream from inside the house. Running back inside, she was met by Polly who told her Mrs Howard had collapsed in the hall.

The housekeeper was lying unconscious near the front door, a large carpet bag clutched in her left hand. Her breathing was very shallow and as Mary knelt beside her, Mrs Howard gave a slight shudder and stopped breathing. Looking up at Polly, Mary could see she understood what had occurred but appeared to be accepting it without undue fuss, so asked her to get Robert and ask him to send James for the doctor.

While Polly was gone, Mary went into the housekeeper's room to collect a sheet to put over the body and was amazed to see the mess Mrs Howard was leaving behind. Mary was in no doubt she was leaving when she collapsed.

Robert accompanied Polly when she returned and he prized the carpet bag handles from Mrs Howard's grasp. They were all shocked to see that as well as a few articles of clothing, the bag was full of silverware. There was also a purse Polly said held the house keeping money for each month, and sure enough it had quite an amount in it. There was also the housekeeping bank book, to which Mrs Howard was a signatory.

Mary asked them both not to say anything about the bag and took it back to the untidy room and locked the door behind her. She then led Polly and Robert to the kitchen for a much needed cup of tea. Mrs Smith was very upset at what had happened, but was even more concerned that Mary was sitting at the servants' table in the kitchen drinking tea from a mug!

Mary asked them to please try to ignore her title for the moment while they discussed the current situation. Despite some initial embarrassment of sitting at the same table with their young mistress, everyone eventually relaxed to a point where they felt comfortable enough to join in the conversation.

Polly said she was in the dining room when she heard Mrs Howard groan before she heard the crash. Mrs Smith added that Mrs Howard had complained to her earlier in the morning that she had a terrible headache.

To take their minds off the tragedy, Mary asked each one to explain their job and the duties they were expected to undertake, then explained that the whole servant system was totally new to her as was the title she now possessed.

She told them that when she landed in England, she had absolutely no idea of her family title and all it concerned, and that she was struggling to come to grips with the formality she now had to deal with.

Dr Wilson arrived mid-afternoon to sign the death certificate and to arrange for Mrs Howard's body to be removed by the undertaker. He said she appeared to have had a massive seizure.

Mary spent the rest of the day in the sitting room, thinking that in a way, this tragedy might be a chance for her to be more involved in running the household, as obviously the indoor servants needed direction until a new housekeeper was employed. She just wanted the servants to accept her without the abject servility she had encountered so far.

Even Mrs Smith appeared to accept the more relaxed attitude as the day wore on, so Mary asked her to just prepare some sandwiches for dinner. She had told the servants they could have light duties for the rest of the day while they dealt with the shock of the housekeeper's sudden death.

Mr Lyons arrived the next morning; James having told Mrs Lyons the news when he passed their house on the way back home. Mary told him of her thoughts about running the household herself until a new housekeeper could be employed. At first he was shocked at the idea, but after Mary explained her need for something to do as she came to grips with the massive change in her life, he began to realise how hard it must be for a young girl, with no previous training for the formal role she was being forced to undertake.

As he admitted, there were no laws stopping a Countess having a hands-on role of running the household. As to the formal role she would be expected to undertake in the community, he decided he needed to find someone who could help her learn what was expected by her peers.

When he was leaving after lunch, Mr Lyons said he would try to find Mrs Howard's next of kin and would arrange the funeral accordingly. He also said his wife was sure to know of women who might be suitable to employ as housekeeper. They decided not to make a fuss of Mrs Howard's apparent attempt to abscond with the silver and housekeeping money.

CHAPTER 8

Following Mr Lyon's departure, Mary called all the servants into the servants' hall at the end of the kitchen, to tell them her plans. From that day on, they would be referred to as staff—not servants—and while she recognised and planned to keep the servant hierarchy, she expected everyone to work together and respect each other.

Mrs Smith would still be in charge of the kitchen and she and Mary would consult daily to plan meals and the kitchen budget. Jane would work with Mrs Smith, and Polly would take instructions from Mary. The outside staff would work as usual.

Mary also told them that while she was keen for them to show respect for her title, and was happy to be called m'lady, she hoped her staff would feel comfortable to talk to her when they met in the house or outside. As she pointed out, they could be respectful without being servile.

She then dropped a bomb shell by saying she would like to eat most of her meals in the servants' hall with her staff. She realised they may be self-conscious with this change to start with, but it made sense when she was the only 'above-stairs' resident.

Apart from the fact it would save Mrs Smith and Jane preparing, cooking and clearing up after double meals, there would be a big saving in the kitchen budget and she wouldn't feel so lonely eating alone in that vast dining room. Another plus would be a greater variety of meals for the staff as she and Mrs Smith would be doing the menu for the staff dinners, not just hers. This brought a murmur of approval from the group.

Of course, if there were visitors, roles would have to become more formal and meals served with the protocol required. However, Mary couldn't see this being a big problem as she had no family that she knew of, nor friends who would visit regularly, if at all.

Leaving the staff to discuss this, Mary went out to the garden then decided to walk around the lake. Fascinated by the numerous birds on the water, Mary walked to the far end of the lake. As she paused to look back at the Hall, she thought she heard a whimper. She couldn't see a dog anywhere nearby, so she started to walk off; but again, she heard the whimper, louder this time.

Looking more closely at the water's edge, she noticed a brown sack half submerged in the water. Quickly, she pulled it out of the lake and discovered to her horror that it contained a small, very wet and cold scruffy grey pup. He felt so cold and lifeless, but as she cuddled him inside her jacket and rubbed him hard, he started to revive to the point he looked at her with big, brown, trusting eyes and then promptly went to sleep.

Mary hurried back to the house with her precious cargo. She asked Polly to get an old towel, and Mrs Smith for some warm milk, and proceeded to rub the puppy hard in front of the fire in the sitting room. Slowly, he started to warm up and dry off to the point where he could sit up and greedily gulp down the warm milk Jane put in front of him. A couple of licks to the hands patting him, and he curled up beside the fire and again went to sleep.

While Polly was dispatched to the laundry to see if she could find an old laundry basket and blanket to make a dog bed, Mary wondered who in the world would tie a helpless little pup in a bag and throw it into the lake. Then she began to wonder: would she be able to keep the puppy and where would he live – in the house or in the outhouse?

With Mrs Smith's consent, Jane was told to keep an eye on the pup while Mary and Mrs Smith consulted on the following week's menu. Both felt it would help take the young girl's mind off the recent tragedy.

Mrs Smith informed Mary that after she left the kitchen following the earlier meeting, everyone had agreed to give Mary's proposal a trial run. They were all very pleased to be called staff instead of servants, and were keen to try to work hard at their jobs without the rigid formality that had been imposed on them throughout their working lives.

Ben arrived mid-afternoon and was surprised to find Mary helping James brush two of the large carriage horses. However, Mr Lyons had told him Mary was struggling to cope with the formality thrust on her, so just greeted them both and said he had a message for Mary from Mr Lyons.

Walking back to the house, Ben told her Mr Lyons had contacted Mrs Howard's brother who lived in Wales. They had arranged for her funeral to take place at the village church at the end of the week. Mr Jones said he and his wife would attend and then take Mrs Howard's possessions back to Wales with them.

Mary and Polly had already packed all of Mrs Howard's clothes and smaller possessions into a chest, and had removed the few pieces of furniture Mrs Smith said belonged to the housekeeper, prior to cleaning the housekeeper's rooms, so Mary was able to inform Ben what would need to be removed. She also issued an invitation to Mr and Mrs Jones to stay at the hall should they wish.

Before he left, Ben told Mary that Mrs Lyons had offered to take her shopping for suitable funeral clothese the next morning.

That night, the staff and Mary, who conceded to sit at the head of the table in the servants hall, were served with a three-course meal of soup, roast beef with all the trimmings, and finally, a large apple pie with cream. Mrs Smith said this was in honour of their new working and dining arrangements, but was quick to add not every dinner would be like this one!

When she went up to bed that night, Mary felt the happiest she had been since her mother's death. She truly felt she could live at the Hall with the support of her staff. Also, she now had some company in her room. Scruffy, as the pup had been named, was curled up in his basket beside the fire. Mary had always had farm dogs for company in Australia and had longed to have one of her own that she could have in the house with her. But Patricia had been adamant that dogs must stay outside. Mary and Scruffy had other ideas.

Mary was woken early the next morning by Scruffy scrabbling at the door. Taking him down to the back courtyard, he happily obliged to do his business, then trotted straight back inside, up the stairs to her bedroom, and onto the bed. Mary concluded any fleas he may have had would have drowned in the lake, so allowed him to cuddle up to her back and went back to sleep.

Breakfast was quite relaxed as the staff discussed their plans for the day. Mary asked them if they would mind using breakfast time as a semi-formal staff meeting when they all could keep each other abreast with jobs needing doing, if extra help was required, etc. Everyone was quite enthusiastic at this new approach to their work.

Robert and Mary set off for Lewes in the buggy straight after breakfast, the horse setting a good pace that covered the six miles in just over half an hour.

Mrs Lyons was a small jovial lady who greeted Mary with such a big smile and friendly approach that Mary instantly felt at ease in her company. Mrs Lyons said she hoped Mary wouldn't mind that her husband had discussed her unexpected elevation into the aristocracy with no formal training, and said she would be only too happy to help Mary whenever she wished.

Robert drove Mary and Celia—as she had been asked to call Mrs Lyons—to a large clothing emporium in the town. There, Mary and Celia spent the next few hours purchasing the type of fashionable clothes that Mary would be expected to wear, not only to the funeral, but also when socialising in her role as Countess.

Mary was pleased to discover Celia had a modern approach to fashions for younger women and could pick out designs that Mary felt reasonably comfortable wearing, but were still fashionable. Thankfully for Mary, she had a figure that allowed her to escape the use of corsets and stays!

At first, Mary was concerned about the amount of money being spent on all this shopping—which also included shoes, hats, under garments and accessories—but was assured by Celia she could afford it with no worries, and all of it was necessary. An account had been set up at the emporium for her which would be paid with the Estate accounts at the end of the month.

All the boxes were to be delivered to the Hall that afternoon, so Mary and Celia retired exhausted for a late lunch at a nearby tea room where once again, it appeared she had an account. Chuckling at Mary's surprise to this revelation, Celia explained that the title of Countess was high up in the aristocratic hierarchy and that any business she chose to deal with would be only too happy to open an account for her.

Before heading home, Mary asked Celia what would be expected of her if Mr Jones and his wife stayed overnight at the Hall. 'Make sure the

servants know what is expected of them and you entertain your guests'
was her reply. 'Don't chatter, let them lead the conversation, but don't
disclose family history or your lack of training.'

As there was no housekeeper, Celia suggested Mary hire a couple
more maids and promote Polly to a more senior maid's role: answering
the front door, monitoring the new maids, etc. If she thought Jane was
up to the job, maybe she could assist as a parlour maid. Celia was sure
there would be some young girls in the village willing to work at the
Hall even for a short period.

The drive back to the Hall was more leisurely than the morning's
drive, and Mary was quite embarrassed to wake up with her head on
Robert's shoulder when the buggy came to a halt at the front steps.

Polly opened the door for Mary as she walked up the steps, and she
was greeted by a grey furry ball tumbling down the steps to meet her.
Scooping him up, Mary gave Scruffy a big hug and was rewarded with
a lick on the nose. He sure doesn't treat me like a Countess, she thought
as he wriggled in her arms.

There was great excitement when the emporium cart delivered
the myriad of parcels soon after their arrival home. Robert had them
stacked in the hallway where Polly and Jane collected them, and took
them up to Mary's dressing room.

Conscious of the necessity to consult with Mrs Smith, partially
in recognition of her more senior position in the indoor staff and also
because she was becoming fond of her cook, Mary went to the kitchen
to discuss the possibility of hiring two more maids. Mrs Smith said she
knew of two sisters in the Village who could help her in the kitchen
and she was sure Jane would be delighted to be allowed 'upstairs' and
out from under her feet all day.

Polly and Jane were called down to the sitting room where they were
told of the possible rearrangement of staff and were delighted, especially
when Mary added they would be getting new, more modern uniforms
as soon as possible. Both found it very hard to contain their excitement
as they went upstairs to help Mary unpack the parcels and put the new
clothing away.

CHAPTER 9

The morning before the funeral, all the staff had breakfast as usual and Mary explained that they would all have to resort to a more formal approach when Mr Jones and his wife arrived later in the morning.

Menus had been arranged, food purchased, and a bedroom prepared for the guests. Mary was probably the most apprehensive of them all, regarding the formality required throughout the visit, whereas all of the present staff were familiar with the protocol. They assured her they would perform as required and maybe, if needed, as unobtrusively as possible, assist Mary if she was at a loss as to what was required in certain circumstances.

The two new maids—twins Sissy and Julie—were to arrive just after breakfast, so the staff suggested they go 'formal' from then on to practice before the guests arrived. When the two young teenage girls arrived, a very formal Polly introduced Mary, using her full title, before escorting them off to the kitchen.

It was all Mary could do to keep a straight face until the door shut behind them. Then she buried her face in a cushion to muffle her laughter, thinking maybe the practice period wasn't such a bad idea after all.

Polly greeted the Jones family when they arrived in the afternoon, announcing them to Mary in the sitting room. Jane brought in a trolley with tea and cake, very self-conscious as she carried out her first official 'upstairs' duty. Thanking her as she left, Mary turned to the family to offer her condolences on their loss.

Mr Jones explained that he hadn't seen his sister for many years but felt they should attend her funeral. He then proceeded to tell Mary a little of their family history and of his job as a Station master in Wales. When he asked Mary had she known his sister for long, she had to explain that she had only just recently arrived at Longmire Hall when Mrs Howard died.

Mary was relieved when Mrs Jones asked could they retire to their room before dinner as they were tired after travelling since before dawn to arrive at Lewes that day, saving her for a time from explaining her new position.

When they had gone upstairs, it suddenly dawned on Mary that she had only been at the Hall for just over a week, but so much had happened in that time she had seen little of the Estate other than her walk to the end of the lake. She knew there were three farms and a village attached to the Estate, but so far, she had only met the two new maids and a couple of people at church. She must remedy that following the funeral.

Dressed in one of her more sombre new dresses, Mary led Mr and Mrs Jones in to dinner, where Polly and Jane, both in their new uniforms, served a magnificent four-course meal, with a solemn Polly keeping an eagle eye on Jane as she carried dishes to and from the table, prompting her softly when required.

As they retired to the sitting room, Mary asked Polly to thank Mrs Smith for the wonderful meal and told Jane she could feed Scruffy some of the left overs, but not bones. Mrs Jones asked who Scruffy was, which led to said pup being allowed into the sitting room to spend the rest of the evening lying near the fire.

Mary hadn't really considered what breed of dog Scruffy was, but Mr Jones said he looked awfully like a friend's Lurcher pup. Thanks to Scruffy, the evening passed quickly with the conversation being mainly about dogs and other family pets.

The next morning, Polly brought a cup of tea up to Mary prior to her breakfast in the breakfast room with her guests. She confirmed that all the staff would be attending the funeral except for Tom and Sam, who would remain to keep an eye on the Hall in their absence.

Robert, resplendent in his formal coachman's uniform, brought the coach with the Countess's insignia on the door, to the front steps. As Mary and the Jones family set off down the drive in the coach, Mrs

Smith, Polly and Jane were being helped onto the jinker by James, also dressed in a new groom's uniform.

Much to Mary's surprise, there were a number of people waiting outside the village church. Ushered to the front pew by the vicar, Mary asked Mr and Mrs Jones to join her. Her staff, she noted, sat near the back.

Following the internment in the graveyard next to the church, the mourners were invited to the Hall for refreshments, so quite a large procession of people followed the coach back to the Hall. James had taken Mrs Smith and the maids home immediately after the service, to give them time to put out the plates of food prepared earlier in the morning. He then very capably stepped up to the roll of Footman, serving drinks to those who preferred an alcoholic drink rather than a cup of tea.

Mary was very proud of her staff's versatility and told them so when she met them in the kitchen after the Jones's had retired to their room.

The next morning, when saying goodbye to the family, Mrs Jones said she had never known gentry she knew treat their servants with such respect as Mary did, and she found it most refreshing. A wink from Polly behind Mrs Jones was nearly Mary's undoing.

When they departed, Mary asked Mrs Smith to join her in the morning room, a delightful smaller room facing east and warmed by the morning sun that streamed in through the French windows leading out into a rose garden. Firstly, Mary thanked Mrs Smith for the wonderful meals she had produced, especially over the past two days. She then asked the cook how long she had been at the Hall and to tell her a little about herself.

Mrs Smith replied that she had been employed at the Hall initially as a twelve-year-old scullery maid forty years ago, and had worked her way up to be a kitchen maid to finally become the cook fifteen years ago. She, like all of the staff who had known her, had loved Lady Patricia and were devastated when she disappeared. They had all had to be very careful when Mr David was home from school because it wasn't just Lady Patricia he was cruel and vindictive to. Everyone was shocked at his death, but not particularly sorry.

To her knowledge, Mrs Smith said she had no family left and now considered the staff at the Hall to be her family. Mary knew Mrs Smith was happy as the cook and ruler of the kitchen, so decided to divulge an idea she had been mulling over since Mrs Howard's death.

Most aristocratic residences with the standing of Longmire Hall had a butler, footmen and housekeeper, plus cook and many maids of various seniority. However, despite being the Countess's residence, Mary said she couldn't see the need, or justify the expense, of a butler or footmen for just her most of the time. Mrs Smith nodded her head and asked what Mary had in mind.

Although Mary had initially thought she could take over some of the housekeeping, she realised she would need to get out to meet people on the Estate and further afield, and also knew she wouldn't be happy kept in the house day on end.

What she was wondering, and needed Mrs Smith's thoughts on, was the possibility of having a combined butler/housekeeper position for front door duties, overseeing the upstairs maids and general housekeeping. This role would be carried out in consultation with Mary and Mrs Smith for financial and budgeting decisions.

Nodding, Mrs Smith supposed it might work but wondered who would agree to a role like that? Mary paused for a moment then asked if she thought Polly would be up for such a role, with their backup of course.

Without pausing to think the matter over, Mrs Smith smiled and said she could think of no one better. Of course, she would need back up but while they were in their 'informal mode' there wouldn't be too much stress from the start.

Over a cup of tea, they then discussed Jane's possible elevation to a permanent upstairs position, with the twins being offered permanent live in positions as kitchen and scullery maids with Mrs Smith. Mary could see Mrs Smith was thrilled to be involved in such a conversation with her, and wasn't surprised when she told her this was the first time she had ever had her opinion sort by the Countess, other than for menu planning.

When Polly was asked would she be interested in the new proposed housekeeper role she was speechless, and begging her lady's pardon, she sat in the nearest armchair. After a few minutes, she stood up and said she would love to give it a try. Jane was similarly thrilled with her promotion.

Mary then went out to the stables to tell Robert, James, and the gardeners of the new indoor staff roles. She then told them that Robert would become the Head Groom/Coachman while James would from now on be the Groom. A new stable hand would be employed when more horses were purchased. The gardening staff would remain as they were for the moment and as before, the outdoor staff would still be involved in the breakfast staff meetings.

CHAPTER 10

Deciding to follow up her earlier plans to buy herself a riding horse, the next morning at breakfast, Mary asked Robert if he knew where they could buy a suitable horse for her. He thought it might take some time to find a suitable horse broken to side-saddle, and was rather taken aback when Mary told him she had only ridden astride in Australia and that she had no intention of ever riding side-saddle.

Listening to her confirmed his opinion that their young Countess had a mind of her own, and was prepared to flout some of the traditional standards. He suggested they might go for a ride on the two bays that morning.

Mary was thankful she had packed her split riding skirt, jacket and riding boots when she left home. Dressing quickly, she almost ran back to the stables, so keen was she to sit on a horse again.

After a quiet greeting with Rusty, the horse James had saddled for her, she accepted his offer of a leg up, though normally she had no trouble mounting a horse by herself. Gathering the reins, she took Rusty for a quiet walk around the courtyard to get the feel of his mouth, and to allow him to adjust to her weight in the saddle.

When Robert mounted Tiger, they walked side by side until they were on the edge of the park, where Robert pointed to a large oak tree in the distance, saying they would ride to it first. Urging Rusty into a gentle canter, Mary found his gait to be quite comfortable, so let him have his head to allow him keep pace with Tiger.

Mary felt exhilarated as the wind whistled past her and at the joy of being on a horse again. When they pulled the horses up at the oak tree, Robert said he was most impressed with her riding and added that Rusty hadn't responded so well with others who had ridden him.

Turning the horses for home after allowing them time to regain their breath, they rode at a more leisurely pace, discussing where they might find a suitable horse for sale. Robert said he would look into it that afternoon.

Mary decided to have a long hot bath when she returned to the house, as she knew she would probably be stiff after being out of the saddle for such a long period. Once she had convinced Scruffy the bath was not for him, she lay soaking till the water started to cool down.

As she was about to get out of the bath, Polly tapped on the door and said she had some warm towels for her. Towelling herself dry with the thick warm towels, Mary began to admit she could maybe get used to this life of luxury!

After church the next day, Robert informed Mary of a local farmer on the other side of the village who had some horses for sale and would be honoured if the Countess would like to look at them. Robert said he was well known for breeding good hunters, not that Mary would have to hunt if she bought one of his horses.

The following day, Robert took Mary in the buggy to Mr Grant's farm about a mile from the village. It had a neat, double storied farm house, large barn, out houses and an impressive stable block.

Both Mr and Mrs Grant came out to greet Mary, and she was invited into the house for a cup of tea. Mrs Grant was so nervous serving a Countess she nearly dropped the teapot, but eventually calmed down so they could enjoy her lovely scones and cake.

Half an hour later, Mary and Robert were taken to the stables, and five horses were paraded before Mary. All were geldings of about sixteen hands, which didn't worry Mary as she had often ridden larger horses. However, none of them made her feel 'that's the one for me.'

As she and Robert were discussing each of the horses, there was a commotion in the stables, a horse neighing loudly and men yelling. Rushing into the stables, Mary saw two men with pitch forks advancing on a dappled grey filly that was rearing as she was forced into an open stall. Mary shuddered as she heard the horse fall backwards in the stall as the door was slammed shut.

Mr Grant explained that she was a rogue horse he had been given to break, but as no one could get near her he was going to have to shoot her. Watching the young filly trembling at the back of the stall, with blood trickling down her chest from a pitch fork prod, Mary's heart went out to the poor animal.

Softly, she started to sing to her soothing words with no real meaning but they appeared to settle the trembling horse. As Mary started to softly call to the horse, she began to take hesitant steps towards the door.

Everyone watching held their breath as Mary gently fondled the muzzle extended towards her, because the horse was known to have a vicious bite. Almost in a dream-like state, the horse allowed Mary to move her hand all over her head, behind her ears, and down her neck. Then, much to everyone's surprise, she stood still to allow Mary to put the halter, that had been hanging near the door, on her.

Mary quietly asked everyone to leave the stable and shut the door as she was going to open the stall door and didn't want the filly to escape if she decided to bolt. When they had done as she asked, she slowly opened the stall door, talking quietly as she did so. The filly followed Mary into the central passage and with a long sigh, put her head on Marys shoulder, almost like saying, 'at last, someone is going to look after me.'

Mary decided there and then that this was to be her horse, even if she wasn't ready to be ridden yet. In Australia, she had taught horses to let her ride them without using the usual method of domination and breaking the horse's spirit. And she was sure she could do the same with this little gem. And that was what she would call her—Gem.

About ten minutes later, Mary called for the door to be opened and she went out with Gem on a lead, walking calmly beside her. When asked if she could buy this horse, Mr Giles was only too happy to be rid of her and asked for her to take her immediately.

So Mary left the farm walking beside the buggy, leading Gem, who was looking around with ears pricked, alert to all going on about her, gently nickering as Mary spoke to her. Robert couldn't believe what he was seeing, after seeing the crazed horse an hour ago.

Mary didn't want to scare Gem by tying her to the buggy so she asked Robert if he thought Rusty would let her ride him while he was in the shafts of the buggy. He wasn't sure but thought it was worth trying, and if anyone could do it he was sure it was Mary.

As he held Gem's lead and Rusty's bridle, Mary sprang onto Rusty's back. After a startled look behind him, he stood still while Robert handed Mary Gem's lead and climbed onto the buggy. After walking out of the farmyard Rusty started to trot briskly towards home with Gem trotting beside him. Mary soon found she could use the shafts a bit like stirrups, making the bare back trot more comfortable.

When they arrived home, everyone was amazed to see their young mistress riding Rusty in the shafts of the buggy, leading a beautiful young grey horse. At her quiet command, they all stood back as she dismounted and Rusty was released from the buggy, then both horses were led into the stables and placed in adjoining stalls.

Mary brushed Gem while James rubbed Rusty down. Both horses were fed and watered, then left contentedly standing close to each other in their stalls.

CHAPTER 11

Early the next morning, Mary went to the stables to find Robert and James quietly talking to Gem, who was standing at the back of her stall. Apparently, she'd had a settled night, but had become frightened when the two men came downstairs from their quarters above the stables.

However, when she saw Mary, Gem walked to the stall door and stood quietly to have her head rubbed. With her hand resting on the young horse's head, Mary asked Robert to come closer and taking his hand, held it for Gem to sniff. With Mary's soft voice encouraging her, she allowed Robert to gently rub her cheek, then her ears.

Mary then called James over and introduced him to the nervous horse. Both men were experienced horse handlers, but were amazed at the way the horse responded to Mary and how she was prepared to accept them so quickly following her quiet introduction. With Mary still near her head, Gem allowed James to enter her stall to place feed in her feed bin.

Shaking his head, Robert asked Mary how she did it, to which she responded she wasn't really sure but it all depended very much on trust. The horse had to trust her, and Mary had to trust the horse not to hurt her. She had always had a special rapport with horses, and people at home had jokingly called her a horse whisperer.

Mary was sure Gem would trust the two men if she didn't feel threatened, as she had been at the Grant's farm. However, she added, she would be happy to be in the stables each morning and at night until the men felt confident Gem trusted them.

As they walked through the back door on their way to the kitchen, Mary noticed a door partially hidden by a small cupboard. Neither men knew where it led to. When Mary asked the rest of the staff, Mrs Smith said it was the indoor entrance to the Estate manager's office, but it had been blocked off since Mr David's death.

Curiosity aroused, Mary decided to have a closer look after breakfast. Everyone was talking about the new horse, but Mary asked them not to go near her until she had settled into her new home. Excusing herself as the staff chatted, Mary walked around the outside of the house until she came to a heavy wooden door with a big metal door knob. Turning it, she found the door to be locked.

Standing on tiptoes, she peered through the small window recessed into the wall and could see a large desk with some papers and books on it, plus cupboards on one wall and a large safe beside a door she assumed was the one she had seen in the passage.

With Polly's help, Mary pulled the cupboard away from the door and found that it was locked. Polly said there were some keys in Mr David's study, a room Mary had not been shown by Mrs Howard. In fact, it dawned on her that there was still a lot of the house she hadn't seen.

Polly explained that the study was very dusty as no one had liked to go into that room following his death. Mary didn't have such qualms and walked in, gazing around at the bookcase on one wall, a well-stocked gun cabinet on the other, and large window looking over the long driveway behind the ornate, flat-topped desk. A couple of sheets of paper and an inkwell were the only items on the desk.

Sitting in the high backed leather chair, Mary tried the drawers on either side of her knees to find all were locked. Frustrated, she turned to look out the window and saw Robert walk across the courtyard. The sun glinted on his watch chain and she had a sudden memory of her father's watch chain that also had some keys on it.

She turned to Polly, still standing at the doorway, and asked her if she knew what had happened to Mr David's personal possessions. As far as Polly was aware, everything was still in his room, the Countess having ordered his room to be left undisturbed.

David's watch chain—with watch and two keys attached—was on the dressing table near his brush set, and a wooden box containing studs, some rings and cravat pins. Taking the keys back to the study, Mary found the first key she tried opened the drawers.

A metal box in a top drawer contained a number of keys, all conveniently labelled with yellow tags. Laying them on the desktop, Mary discovered a key for each of the office doors, plus another larger one named 'Office safe'.

Mary and Polly could hardly contain their excitement as they raced back to the inside door and inserted the key. With little pressure, it turned, and when Mary turned the doorknob, the door opened into the office.

The office was very tidy with a less ornate but larger flat-topped desk, and a leather office chair. The first book opened was a ledger of rents, collected quarterly from the farms and village tenants. By the dates, it looked like the next payments were due in a few days.

Mary had enjoyed doing the bookwork and budgeting on the farm at home, and hoped she might be able to be involved in the Estate bookkeeping. She had yet to meet the Estate manager who was still away from the Estate. The gong sounded for lunch before they could look much further, so everything was left as they found it and they locked the door behind them as they left.

Mary decided to spend some time with Gem after lunch, taking her to the small field behind the stables. At first a little hesitant she followed Mary around the field, occasionally taking a bite of grass as she went. Eventually, she felt comfortable enough to move a little away from Mary, who stood in the middle of the field talking quietly to her. When she felt Gem had relaxed enough, Mary asked Robert to let Rusty loose in the field.

Mary walked to the gate where she and Robert watched the two horses cantering around the field, obviously enjoying the freedom but keeping close to each other. As they watched, a small buggy with a woman at the reins entered the courtyard. Robert explained it was Jess Telford from the Home Farm, before going over to assist her alight prior to introducing her to Mary.

Mary remembered that Mrs Telford and her husband were at the funeral. She led her into the house. On the way in, Mary asked Jane for some tea and cake to be taken to the sitting room. Apologising for calling unannounced, Mrs Telford, who asked to be called Tess, explained that their family was in utter turmoil at the moment as the quarterly rent was due at the end of the week. She was afraid they were not going to be able to pay the increased amount Mr Morris, the Estate manager, had decreed they owed, on threat of instant eviction from the farm should the full amount not be paid at the upcoming rent day.

Tess broke down sobbing, apologising for approaching Mary with the issue, but they didn't know what else to do. Her husband was currently looking at having to sell some of the dairy herd to try to meet the higher rent, and she knew Old Tom on one of the other farms was planning to sell all his cattle and leave.

Mary was appalled to hear that all the tenants on the three farms and in the village had had their rents raised and had similar threats of eviction. When told how much the Telfords were expected to pay, Mary excused herself to go to the office and check the rent ledger she had seen on the desk earlier.

As she thought, the amount Tess had told her was nearly double the amount listed in the ledger. All the rents listed were of varying amounts for different tenants, but as far as Mary could see, all tenants had had a regular quarterly payment for the past few years. What was going on?

Hurrying back to the sitting room, Mary was pleased to see that Tess had composed herself and asked her to tell her a little about her family and the Home Farm. Tess and Bob, her husband, had taken over the Home Farm from Bob's father who had lived there from the time Bob's grandfather had taken on the tenancy of the farm. Tess said she had three children, two sons in their early twenties, and a younger son of sixteen.

They were hoping that Will, their eldest son, would take over from them when he was older. They owned their own dairy herd—some sheep, pigs and cattle, and supplied the Hall with meat, milk, butter, cheese and eggs—their rent being adjusted to cover payment for these supplies.

When Tess left, having been told by Mary that she would look into the matter and also having been assured that they would not be evicted by Mr Morris, Mary went back to the office. She looked through the desk drawers and the cupboards on the wall, finding nothing she considered untoward. Just Agricultural books, leaflets, bank receipts for money paid into the Estate bank account and invoices from the numerous vendors with whom the Estate dealt with.

However, when she opened the safe, she discovered a newer ledger with all the tenants listed, with higher rental amounts next to their names. These figures were for quarterly payments dated from just before David died, the amounts increasing each quarter. Money paid and upcoming rent was listed, plus there was an additional listing of payments from an address in London.

It appeared that each tenant's rent would have doubled in twelve months when the next rents were paid. There was also a cash box containing a large sum of money, and pushed right to the back of the safe was a bank book in the name of Anthony Morris with some large deposits listed.

Sitting at the desk comparing the amounts in both ledgers, Mary began to suspect that the deposits in the bank book were similar to the difference between the amounts listed in the ledgers. It looked very much as though Mr Morris was embezzling the extra money he was collecting in rents each quarter.

Mary decided she should show the ledgers and bank book to Mr Lyons the next day, if possible. As she had no idea when Mr Morris would return, she jammed the outside door so it could not be opened, then pulled the cupboard back against the hallway door after locking it, hoping Mr Morris didn't have that key.

That evening, during dinner, Mary asked the staff if they had heard of the increased rents in the village. Tilly said their parents' rent had gone way up and their parents were really worried about Mr Morris's next visit, and so were their neighbours. Robert said he was also aware of concern of possible evictions in the village.

Mary told Robert she wished to leave for Lewes immediately after breakfast the next morning, and asked James if he felt comfortable spending some time with Gem by himself. He replied he would be happy to as he was becoming very fond of the young filly, and she seemed quite happy when he was near her.

CHAPTER 12

When Robert dropped Mary off at the solicitor's' office the next morning, she was ushered straight in to see Mr Lyons. When she showed him the two ledgers and bank book, and told him of her suspicions he was horrified at what appeared to be embezzlement of funds, not just from the Estate but from the tenants as well. He told her Mr Morris, a friend of David's, had been appointed not long before David's death, but he hadn't seen him much since David's funeral.

So long as he collected, registered and payed the required amount into the Estate account, he was pretty much a free agent, travelling between the three properties, arranging for repairs as required. At no time had he informed Mr Lyon's office of the increased rents. He had heard a rumour the Estate manager was spending quite a lot of time lately at the London residence, instead of at his cottage on the Estate, but had not been unduly concerned.

What were the sums of money from the London residence, he wondered? The butler and his wife had a set budget for keeping the house ready—should her Ladyship wish to visit London—and they sent their accounts to Mr Lyon's office to be paid, so there should be no additional money going into anyone's bank account.

He asked for Mary's permission to keep the ledgers and bank book for the rest of the day, to spend more time comparing them with the Estate accounts, and also to possibly show them to the Police. Mary agreed, though expressed her concern that should Mr Morris return before they were returned to the office, he would be alerted that someone had been in the office.

Mr Lyons immediately set three of his office staff to copying all relevant pages so Mary and Robert could return to the Estate after they had a short lunch. He said he would come out to the Hall later the next morning to report on progress, and maybe offer some plans of action.

Mary was relieved to get everything back in the office and unjam the outside door when they arrived home, then she went out to spend the rest of the afternoon in the paddock with Gem, getting her used to being handled out of her stall and gently introducing her to the lunge rope. At feed time she trotted over to James, who was watching near the gate and followed him into the stable.

The following morning, Mr Lyons arrived and told Mary of his visit to the Police, the Estate's bank manager, and the manager of Mr Morris's bank account. The police suggested they supply Bob Telford with bank notes, with the numbers listed, to pay the rent on the day it was due.

When the final tenant had left the Estate office, the police would go in and check the ledgers and the safe. Mr Lyons had arranged to record the note numbers and suggested he and Mary go to the Home Farm straight away to discuss the plan with Bob and Tess.

The Telfords were thrilled and very relieved that Mary and Mr Lyons were putting a plan into place to stop them from being evicted from their farm. Mary and Mr Lyons were invited to lunch, and it was a very jovial meal. Mary was introduced to the three sons—Will, Matthew, and John. Both younger boys were currently working part time next door, helping Old Joe with his cattle. Mary found it a little disconcerting having boys about her own age all being so subservient towards her.

On their way back to the Hall, Mary asked Mr Lyons if he would mind calling on Old Joe so she could tell him he would not be required to sell his herd to pay his rent. While relieved to hear this, and promising not to spread the news, Joe told her he was finding the farm too much work with his arthritis and would like to eventually sell his cattle to allow him to move closer to his daughter near Brighton.

This started Mary thinking, and she asked Mr Lyons if it would be possible for her to buy his cattle and employ workers, rather than leasing the farm to another tenant. He told her that it would be possible, and asked if she had anyone in mind. From her earlier conversation with Tess, Mary knew that the two younger sons were looking for more work as there wasn't really a living for them on the Home Farm, and suggested she offer them jobs as full-time paid employees to run the second farm.

When Mr Lyons returned to Lewes, Mary had James saddle Tiger and she rode over to the Home Farm to discuss her plans with Bob and Tess. They thought it would be the answer to their prayers to keep the boys employed near home. Will was consulted, and agreed it would do the two younger boys good to work for themselves, but they would be near enough to help each other as needed.

When Matt and John were asked, they were ecstatic, though Mary had to restrain their enthusiasm, saying she had to discuss the proposition with Joe and get his agreement before they could start on their own.

As Mary rode next door, she thought this was the sort of work the Estate manager should be doing, certainly not someone in her new position. However, she shrugged her shoulders and decided she would do what she wanted to, within reason of course. It was a lovely day for a ride and she was thoroughly enjoying the sun on her back.

Old Joe was overjoyed at her proposition, and was pleased to hear that Matt and John would be taking over the farm he had loved and tendered nearly all his working life. Mary asked him to find out at the market what a fair price would be for his cattle, and said she would consult Bob about the prices he would offer if he was buying Joe's other goods and chattels. She also told him he was not expected to pay any more rent.

CHAPTER 13

The day before rent day, everyone was on tenterhooks awaiting the arrival of Mr Morris. Usually, he was on the Estate well before rent day, but he had been away for so long no one knew when he would arrive. He must know by now that a new Countess had been found, and whether that would make him stay away—or if he would just take the contents of the safe and run—nobody was sure.

He would know though, that this rent day would be the last chance to make a lot of extra money and might gamble on the fact that she was not yet in residence, or at least would not deign to be involved with the tenants. Mr Lyons suggested Mary not be introduced to Mr Morris when he arrived, and all the staff were keen to play along with the plan to keep Mary's whereabouts a secret when he arrived.

Mid-afternoon, Mary was in the hall talking to Polly when they heard a horse galloping down the drive. Looking through the front window, they saw a large man whipping his lathered horse, which made Mary's blood boil. Just before she could open the front door to yell at him, Polly grabbed her arm and told her it was Mr Morris. Although still seething at the ill treatment of his horse, Mary ran upstairs to her bedroom as had been decided, while Polly went to warn Jane and the kitchen staff.

Not long afterwards, the back door burst open and Mr Morris barged into the kitchen, pushing Sissy against the wall as he strode past. He was a big man with a bald head and a shaggy beard, which Polly told Mary later on, looked like his hair had slipped down his head. He bellowed for a cup of tea and something to eat, and slapped at Julie as she moved past him to pour water into the tea pot.

From past experience, Mrs Smith knew there was little use trying to stop him being so rough with the girls, as he had knocked her over a couple of times in the past when no one was watching. He had always been a bad-tempered bully, so she wasn't surprised at his ill humour, as she was sure there would have some jeering as he rode through the village.

Mr Morris lived in one of the cottages near the stables, and there was great relief when he informed Mrs Smith that he would not be requiring dinner or breakfast as he had brought some food with him. Taking fresh milk, cheese and tea from the kitchen, he went over to his cottage and was later seen entering the Estate office with his saddle bags over his shoulder.

Dinner that night was a sombre affair, with Mary eating in her room and James in the stables, keeping a watch on the office door. Robert said they had set up a roster to keep an eye on the cottage all night and he would make sure no horse could be taken from the stables that night, should Mr Morris decide to bolt. The gatekeeper had also been warned not to open the gates for anyone and to stay out of sight, opening the gates only when Robert told him to do so in the morning.

Rent day dawned as an overcast, drizzly day, in keeping with the mood of the tenants as they gathered in the courtyard to pay their rent. Mr Morris walked across to the office five minutes before the first tenant was summoned to enter.

Each tenant's time in the office was very short, only long enough for Mr Morris to count the money, check it off against the tenant's name and have them sign the ledger—or as in most cases to make their mark—before they were curtly told to leave.

The next person had to wait a number of minutes before they were called in to go through the same process. Mrs Smith kept the waiting men supplied with hot tea and scones, though some were grumbling that the Countess should do more than that. Mary was being held responsible for the higher rents and the suffering they had to endure to try to scrape together the money demanded.

All of the tenants assumed she would just allow things to carry on as they had since Mr David had become more involved in running the

Estate as his mother grew older. Only the Telfords and Old Joe knew of the fraudulent rise in rents and what was to happen later that day.

A couple of men who hadn't managed to produce the higher rent came out looking stunned, having been told they were to be out of their cottages at the end of the week. Mary had instructed Robert to quietly move any tenants threatened with eviction away from the group as quickly as possible to stop more unrest, and to take them home after explaining that the Countess would not allow the eviction to be carried out.

Bob Telford was one of the last to enter the office and said later that Mr Morris had appeared quite disappointed when he counted out the correct amount, as though he had been looking forward to telling him to leave the Home Farm.

When the last tenant left, Mr Morris locked himself in the office and spent the next half hour in there alone, before coming out with his saddlebags hung over his shoulder. As he locked the door behind him, the two police constables, who had been waiting in the stables, walked up to Mr Morris and pushed him up against the door.

While one policeman removed the saddle bags from the agent's shoulder and the key from his hand, the other burley policeman snapped a pair of handcuffs on Mr Morris's left wrist and pushed him into the office where he was shackled to a chair to await Mary's and Mr Lyons' arrival.

Mr Lyons had joined Mary just before the last tenant had paid his rent, so they entered the office together in time to hear Mr Morris proclaiming his innocence for whatever the constables thought he had done. He barely gave Mary a glance as he demanded that Mr Lyons tell him what was going on.

Without answering, Mr Lyons opened the ledger on the desk to the latest entries for the current rent day, each showing the lower rents with the tenants' signature or mark in the column beside their name and the amount paid. While he scanned the ledgers, Mary opened the safe and found the cashbox with the money to go into the Estate account, tallied to the amount the lower rents added up to, with a bank payment form filled out ready to go to the bank the next day, as was the usual practice.

Emptying the contents of the saddle bags onto the desk, Mr Lyons showed the policemen the newer ledger with the higher rents as paid that day and signed by each tenant. A leather pouch contained the excess money paid by each tenant, some of the notes being those paid by Bob Telford.

There was also a payment form made out to Mr Morris's bank account for the money in the pouch, plus an additional amount in another purse that tallied with a new notation against the London address. The bank book and an amount of money that was similar to the money Mary and Mr Lyons had seen in the safe earlier was found in Mr Morris's Jackt pocket.

A sullen agent was bundled onto the cart Robert had waiting in the courtyard, and was driven off to the Lewes police cells. Mr Lyons accepted Mary's offer to stay overnight; Robert being asked to pass the message to Mrs Lyons and to collect an overnight case for him before returning from Lewes.

Mary was amazed at how easily the staff snapped into formal mode, much better than she felt she did, when told Mr Lyons would be staying the night. He was quite amused at the transformation, knowing Mary's usual informality with her staff.

He commented after the evening meal, served in the dining room by Polly and Jane, that he had truly believed her less formal approach with her servants would have led to less care in their work and possible disrespect towards Mary and her visitors. However, he was beginning to see that the staff, as he now agreed to call them, were happier in their work and trying hard to do their best to please Mary, for whom he believed they had the utmost respect, even after such a short period.

Mary was well aware of the simmering resentment towards her from the villagers, due to the higher rents they were being forced to pay. This money—Mr Lyons assured Mary—would be put into the Estate account after Mr Morris was tried for fraud and robbery. The rest of the evening, Mr Lyons and Mary spent discussing how to deal with the excess rent and the money in Mr Morris's bank account which appeared to be the excess amount collected since David's death.

Mr Lyons also told Mary he had heard back from the private detective he had sent to London, when he saw the additional money listed in the ledger accredited to the London residence. Apparently, Mr Morris, the butler and his wife, had been leasing out rooms to younger sons of the aristocracy who needed a London address for periods of time. They provided breakfast but all other meals were sort elsewhere. It was quite a lucrative business, with a long waiting list. Mr Lyons was prepared to go to London to dismiss the butler and his wife, if Mary agreed.

That night, Mary lay in bed thinking about the illegal business being carried out in the London residence, which she had yet to visit. She wondered what would be required to make the business legal and make the residence a profitable business for the Estate, rather than a drain on its finances.

CHAPTER 14

The Sunday following rent day, Mary asked the Vicar if she could speak to the congregation before they left the church. Although a little nervous when the Vicar announced that Lady Mary wished to speak to the congregation, Mary stood up and first of all apologised for the way the tenants had been treated over the past two years, as their rents were increased and the threat of possible eviction was held over their heads.

She also told them she was sorry she had been unable to ease their fears before the last rent day—knowing some were going hungry to scrape together the due amount—because the Police needed to catch Mr Morris red-handed with their money to enable them to arrest him and seize the money he had collected.

When Mary spoke of her plans to return all the excess rent paid by the tenants after the trial, there were at first murmurs of disbelief, then everyone stood up and cheered when she told them of her other proposal.

Mary told the congregation that there would be a bag of flour delivered to each tenant's household, plus the Estate would pay up to £12/household to the village butcher and up to £10/household to the grocer—to be rationed on a weekly basis for the next quarter— according to the size and also to the earning capacity of each family. In addition, a load of coal would be delivered to each household for the winter.

The whole congregation continued to clap and cheer as Mary and the Vicar proceeded them from the church. Once outside in the sunshine, every man and woman bowed or curtsied to Mary and thanked her for her generous offer.

Finally, when Mary was able to make her way out of the churchyard, she decided to walk back to the Hall with the staff, who were basking in the goodwill now being bestowed on their mistress. The twins in particular were ecstatic as they knew how much Mary's offer would mean to their family.

A couple of mornings later, as Mary lay in bed, she realised she still hadn't seen the rooms on the floors above hers, nor had she been to the village other than to the church. Time to slow down and get her bearings and meet more of the people on the Estate.

After working Gem for an hour that morning, Mary decided to try putting a bridle on her. As she had hoped, Gem accepted it without any sort of irritation or discomfort. She even allowed Mary to lie across her back, much to the disbelief of Robert who held the bridle. He had never seen a horse trained to take a rider this way, and wouldn't have believed it if he hadn't seen it with his own eyes.

Mary was thrilled at Gem's progress and felt she might soon be ready to allow her to sit on her back. However, she didn't want to push the young filly too fast. Scruffy seemed to sense Mary's elation when she went into the house, racing backwards and forwards, attacking her feet as she walked, then racing off to get a toy for her to throw.

He had grown in the short time since she found him and was becoming a much-loved member of the household. He adored Mary and followed her everywhere. He was a quick learner and knew that he wasn't to go near the horses. When Mary was with Gem, Scruffy lay patiently outside the fence, not moving until Mary called him.

Mary told Polly she could move down from her room in the attic to the Housekeeper's rooms, so after lunch, Polly and Jane spent the afternoon cleaning Polly's new rooms, while Mary and Scruffy set off to explore the rooms upstairs.

She was surprised to find an additional five large bedrooms as well as the nursery, which consisted of the schoolroom, a small sitting room, nursery maid's bedroom, governess's bedroom and sitting room, plus five smaller children's bedrooms around the corner—each with a large single bed, chest of drawers, wardrobe and desk.

There were steep, narrow stairs going up to the attics and down to the kitchen at one end of the nursery next to a bathroom, which Mary assumed must be for the staff who slept in the attic rooms, while the bathroom at the other end of that wing would be for the children and nursery/school staff.

On a lower shelf of the bookshelf, Scruffy found a toy pig which he gently took in his mouth and pranced around Mary, before galloping down the stairs to show it to everyone else. Mary followed more slowly and asked Polly and Jane if she could have a look at the attic rooms, when they went up to collect Polly's possessions and clean her room.

Sounds of singing were drifting up from the kitchen and Mary thought how much happier the staff were, smiling as they worked and often helping each other with jobs, whereas a few weeks ago they weren't even allowed to speak to each other when they were working and were constantly in fear of suffering the wrath of the housekeeper.

The twins were a breath of fresh air in the kitchen, sharing the jobs of kitchen and scullery maid amid peals of laughter, and quite often somewhat tuneless duets. Mrs Smith was revelling in their company, as well as her daily chats with Mary to plan dinner menus.

The entire staff were thrilled with the variety of evening meals being served, and all were enjoying the less formal approach to their work and to each other, although they were always polite and respectful to Mary when in her company.

When Mary and the two maids made their way up to the attics, she was surprised at the number of doors along the passage. However, when she saw the size of the rooms, she understood how there could be so many rooms on that floor.

Many were being used as storerooms, others were totally bare, and five were currently the bedrooms of the female staff. Each room had a sloping ceiling and a small window, with only just enough room for a single bed and a wash stand with a jug and basin, plus a small set of drawers.

Polly said that in summer the rooms were very hot and airless, as many of the windows didn't open, while in winter the rooms were freezing and damp.—In fact, Mrs Smith had told them she had ice on her blanket one winter, before some roof repairs had been carried out several years ago.

Compared with the proportions of all the other rooms and staircases she had seen in the house, Mary was appalled at the basic sleeping quarters of her staff, who, after long hours of hard work were expected to climb to the top of the multi-storied house up a very steep, narrow, wooden staircase.

She was beginning to realise that many women and men in service were seen and treated as chattels by their employers, with little to no thought of their comfort and well-being other than that they could carry out the duties set for them. If they couldn't, they were quickly replaced.

Later that evening, Mary asked Mrs Smith if there was any ruling that live in staff, other than a butler or housekeeper, had to sleep in the attics, to which the cook replied that it was just a cheap convenient way to keep staff apart from and out of sight of the family living in the house.

Mary thought about this, then asked Mrs Smith if she would like to move to the governess's bedroom and sitting room. The incredulous look on the cook's face made Mary laugh, then she realised that to have a larger room 'downstairs' to herself with a fireplace was beyond Mrs Smith's wildest dreams.

Mary then told Jane and the twins they could move to the children's rooms, which were larger, more insulated, and each had a small fireplace for heating. She planned for the move to take place the next day after the rooms had been prepared for the new occupants.

The next morning, while the excited women cleaned their new rooms, Mary and Robert took Gem out into the small field for some lunging work. There, much to everyone's surprise, Gem not only allowed Mary to lie across her back as she had the day before but also stood still while Mary slowly swung her right leg over her back and sat up.

All the time, Mary spoke softly to the young horse whose ears flicked backwards and forwards as she listened intently. Gem looked around as Mary sat up, then walked quietly around the field with Robert walking near her head, his hand lightly resting on her neck.

After about ten minutes of walking and trotting, Mary dismounted and hugged Gem, as Robert shook his head in disbelief. Never had he seen an unbroken horse allow a rider on its back without bucking and trying to throw the rider off.

The next few days were spent much more quietly than the previous two weeks, the staff settling into their new quarters, and happily going about their duties. Mary spent a lot of time riding Gem, who didn't appear to be worried by the light saddle she now wore when being ridden.

In fact, she seemed to revel in their rides around the park. Scruffy had been accepted as a riding companion, provided he stayed away from her hooves and the three of them spent many pleasant hours together out in the fresh air and sunshine. Gem and Rusty still spent time together, but Gem appeared to be happiest when she was near Mary.

Two weeks later, the trial of Anthony Morris was held at the Longmire Court of assizes, where he was charged with embezzlement and fraud. Mary was called as a witness, and was treated with great deference when she entered the court house.

It took a very short time for Mr Morris to be found guilty of both charges, and he was sentenced to twelve years imprisonment at Reading Prison. All bank accounts in his name were confiscated by the court and the misappropriated money was to be returned to Lady Mary to do with as she wished.

Following the trial, Mary was invited to lunch in the Judge's chambers where she was introduced to several members of the local legal fraternity. All professed their gratitude for her speed in notifying Mr Lyons of her suspicions that led to Mr Morris being apprehended, an act they often found sadly lacking when dealing with many of the aristocracy.

After lunch, the Judge asked Mary if she was aware that as a Peer of the Realm, she was entitled and expected to be a local Magistrate. Chuckling at the shocked look on her face, he explained that she would not be required to take up her duties until she was twenty-one in a couple of years.

He told her he would be honoured to coach her in the duties she would be expected to undertake, and to give her some instruction in English law. He also assured her that she would not be expected to reside in court alone until she felt confident to do so.

A rather bewildered Mary rode back to Longmire in the carriage, wondering what else was in store for her.

CHAPTER 15

As life started to settle into a more regular pattern for Mary, she had more time to survey her new domain. She spent time with Polly going through each floor and wing of the Hall, discussing how best to deal with the vast number of unused rooms.

Many of the bedrooms were shut, as were the ballroom and two of the reception rooms, thus requiring less cleaning, until required for future formal occasions. Mary also decided to only use the dining and sitting rooms when visitors called and to refurbish the study for her personal use. Although a smaller room in the Hall, it was still larger than the living room back on the farm in Australia.

Once the study had been thoroughly cleaned, two comfortable lounge chairs were placed on either side of the fireplace. The desk, bookcase and gun cabinet remained in place, cleaned and polished.

In the absence of an Estate agent, Mary had started to keep the books, checking invoices and paying bills. At first, she started working in the Estate office, but once the study was available, she did most of the bookwork at the study desk. If tenants called to discuss issues, they met Mary in the Estate office.

Mary finally managed to visit Glendale, the third farm on the Estate, after the tenant Thomas Grey called to ask for some help in repairing his barn that had been damaged in a recent storm. Glendale was a larger farm than Home farm and Farm two, situated in the higher country of the Estate. Thomas and his brother Paul, with the help of four shepherds, ran large flocks of Suffolk and Border Leicester sheep in the hills.

Robert accompanied Mary when she rode to Glendale, explaining that the shepherds slept in small huts dotted around the hills as they followed their flocks that grazed the hillsides for about nine months of the year, moving down near the house in the winter when the hills were covered with snow.

Mary had never seen snow, so had little concept of the hardships it caused for hill farmers like Thomas and Paul. However, she listened carefully to Robert's explanation and was quick to ask questions if she didn't understand. By the time they reached the valley where the house was situated, Mary felt she understood most of what Robert had said, but was totally unprepared for the sight that beheld her as they topped the rise overlooking the house and farmyard.

The house was a very small thatched cottage, built right against a large boulder in the side of the hill. Attached to the side of the cottage was a large barn and several out buildings enclosed the small farmyard. The end of the barn furthest from the cottage had been crushed by a large boulder that had rolled down the hill.

Both Thomas and Paul were in the yard as Mary and Robert rode in. As they dismounted, two large, shaggy black and white sheepdogs raced into the yard, barking furiously. At Mary's quiet command, they sat quietly in front of her, leaving Thomas and Paul staring in amazement. Thomas apologised, saying they normally tied the dogs up when they knew visitors were coming, but hadn't realised her Ladyship was riding up to see them so soon after his visit to the Hall.

Mary explained that in the absence of an Estate manager she was dealing with the Estate affairs, and was keen to familiarise herself with as much of the Estate as she could. This was much easier to accomplish riding Gem than being shaken about in a carriage.

As Paul took the horses into the stable, Mary asked if she could look around the barn and out buildings before going inside. Poor Thomas could only nod his head, as he had never known a lady, let alone a Countess, interested in being in a messy farmyard and its buildings. Taking pity on him, Mary told him a little of her farming experiences in Australia, and her desire to learn a lot more about farming in England.

Mary was fascinated to see the barn was divided into many small pens. Seeing Mary's interest, Thomas slowly overcame his embarrassment and explained that the pregnant ewes were brought into the barn to lamb when it was snowing. Thomas and Paul took it in turns to sleep in the barn during lambing, in order to assist ewes if required. The other sheep were kept in sheltered fields near the farmyard during the winter, to make it easier to feed them and monitor the new lambs.

Hay and grain was stored in the far end of the barn where the roof gaped open. Obviously, repairs needed to be carried out as soon as possible to stop the rain from ruining the stored feed supplies, so essential for later in the year.

Mary knew that normally an Estate Agent would organise the repairs, but in the absence of such she asked Thomas to tell her what needed to be done to repair the barn and what needed to be done to protect the fodder in the interim. With this information written in her notebook, Mary had a quick look at the other buildings, noting that as they came closer to the cottage, both Thomas and Paul were becoming more and more anxious.

Assuming they were embarrassed to have her in their cottage, Mary asked would it be possible to sit on a bench at the side of the building and have a cool drink of water while enjoying the sunshine. She had to smother a smile at the look of relief on their faces.

Both dogs lay at her feet, having walked beside her on their tour of the farm buildings, often with their muzzles pressed into her hand when she stopped to look at something. Paul said he had never seen them be so friendly, even to himself or his brother.

Before riding away from Glendale, Mary assured the Grey brothers that she would get work started on the barn as quickly as possible. In the meantime, she would have a large tarpaulin sent up to cover the fodder as a short term protection from rain.

On the way back to the Hall, Mary called in at Home Farm, while Robert went back to the stables. Mary sought Bob's advice on potential workers in the village who would be capable of carrying out the repairs, and where she might source the materials needed. He told her he was going to Lewes market the next day, and could speak to a couple of tradesmen who he was sure would be pleased to give her an assessment and quote for the materials needed.

The next morning, Mary walked to the village where she was now a very welcome visitor. As she walked along the street, she was given a cheerful greeting from all she met and she stopped many times to enquire of the welfare of family members.

Eventually, she spoke to the four men Bob had mentioned, and offered them the job of repairing the Glendale barn. All accepted immediately, saying they would be happy to start as soon as the materials were delivered. Mary knew that several of her tenants in the village were struggling to find lasting work in the district, and she was determined to help them as much as she could.

She was pleased to hear that the two Telford boys she employed were working hard on Old Joe's farm, and that they were sowing new crops and repairing fences and buildings in preparation to purchasing more cattle to run on the property. Maybe they would need some extra help soon.

CHAPTER 16

One cool morning in late June, as Mary, Gem, and Scruffy were returning from a ride on the Estate, Scruffy suddenly dived into a dense bush and started to bark. Thinking he had bailed up a fox, she whistled to him and was about to ride on when a small boy ran out screaming.

Jumping from Gem, Mary grabbed the boy before he could run away and held him to her until he stopped struggling. As she held him, he started sobbing and said his brother was being eaten by a wolf. Hurrying back to the bush, still holding the young boy, she shouted to Scruffy to come immediately which he did, then stood whimpering as he stared at the bush. Telling him to be quiet, Mary could hear sobbing.

Letting go of the boy, she pushed her way through the low branches to find a younger boy curled up with one arm wrapped around his head, sobbing uncontrollably. His thin grubby shirt was bloody on the back and he was shaking, from cold or fright, Mary wasn't sure. Probably both. Taking off her coat, she placed it over the sobbing boy and backed out of the bush, telling him she would be back soon.

She wrapped her jacket around the other boy and swung him up onto Gem's back before he realised what was happening, then mounted behind him. Gem turned her head with a surprised look, but with gentle encouragement from Mary, she stood still. Scruffy was ordered to stay guard, Mary praying he wouldn't follow as she turned Gem towards home, hugging the young boy to her as she urged Gem into a gallop.

Robert and James ran out of the stables, and Tom and Sam appeared in the courtyard as they heard Gem galloping towards the Hall. Quickly, Mary handed the boy down to Tom, telling him to take him straight to the kitchen to warm him up and not to let him out of his sight till she returned.

She briefly explained what she'd found and asked James to ride to Lewes immediately for Dr Wilson, and Robert to follow her with the cart. While he harnessed the horse, she grabbed an old coat from the tack room then set off on Gem back to where she had left Scruffy and the second boy. Scruffy was very pleased to see her and enjoyed her praise for staying when she rode off.

There was no sound from the bushes but a quick look showed the boy had not moved. He was barely conscious when Robert arrived and crawled in and slid him onto Mary's coat. Together they slowly pulled him out, wrapped him in the coat and lay him in the back of the cart. Gem was tied to the cart and Mary sat in the back holding the boy as they made their way back to the Hall. All the staff, except Tom, were waiting at the back door when they arrived in the courtyard.

Robert carefully carried the boy into the kitchen and placed him on a small mattress Mrs Smith had had placed near the stove, to warm him up and reunite him with his brother who was almost asleep on Tom's lap as he sat in Mrs Smith's armchair. Tom told Mary that the boy he held was Alfie, and his brother on the mattress was Jack. All they could get from Alfie was that Jack had been whipped and had broken his arm.

Mrs Smith had given Alfie a drink of hot chocolate and he had eaten a bowl of bread and warm milk before sitting with Tom near the fire. As Jack lay wrapped in a blanket on the mattress, Alfie scrambled down and cuddled up to him, and so they stayed until the doctor arrived.

In the meantime, Mrs Smith turned her attentions to Mary—who was obviously chilled to the bone from riding in the cold without jacket or warm coat—making her sit in the other chair near the stove with a blanket around her shoulders and plying her with a hot mug of tea with some brandy in it.

About half an hour later, Dr Wilson arrived, James having met him on his way home from a visit to a patient on the other side of the Estate. Dr Wilson was horrified to see Jack's back when his shirt had been gently eased off. His whole back and buttocks were criss-crossed with angry red welts, many of them still seeping blood. He gently bathed all the wounds with warm water mixed with some antiseptic from his bag, and then added some salve and covered it with a piece of clean sheet. He then straightened the obviously broken arm, thankful his young patient was unconscious, and bound it with a splint and bandages.

After checking Alfie and announcing he would be fine after a hot bath and some good nourishing food, Dr Wilson took Mary aside and told her he had heard that the two young boys were missing from the Workhouse in town. Mary asked him to please not report their whereabouts until they found out how Jack had received his injuries. Agreeing to wait until he returned the next day, he left with instructions that Jack would need to be watched throughout the night, even after he regained consciousness.

Jack was put to bed in the room next to Mary's, and Polly agreed to sit with him while Alfie was given a long hot bath and a big bowl of vegetable soup with a chunk of bread and cheese. Clad in one of Robert's old shirts that came down to below his knees, he climbed into bed beside Jack and immediately fell asleep. Scruffy would have happily joined them, but was ordered out to his bed downstairs.

Jack recovered consciousness later in the afternoon and after a small serving of soup and a dose of laudanum Dr Wilson had left, he fell asleep. Both boys woke in the evening, ate some stew, and then went back to sleep, cuddled together in the thick feather mattress. So far, nothing more had been said about who they were or where they had come from.

Polly, Jane, and the twins took turns to sit with the boys during the night, having convinced Mary she should have a good night's sleep following her chilly experience in the morning, saying they couldn't look after her too if she caught a chill. Despite her reluctance to leave the work to the four staff, she was secretly thrilled that they were genuinely concerned for her well-being, and more so that they were prepared to ignore her title and treat her as someone they respected and cared for.

Alfie came down to breakfast the next morning, wrapped in Polly's dressing gown and ate a big bowl of porridge and some toast before he hesitantly told Mary and the staff that he was almost ten and Jack was eight. They had been sent to the Workhouse when he was six after their parents had died of typhoid. The Supervisor and his wife, the Matron, were kind to them and made sure they were not picked on and they settled in quite well.

However, a few months ago, when the Supervisor died, a new man and his wife took over. They were very strict and beat the children for any perceived misdemeanour, restricting meals to two per day and cutting the rations to the point the children were nearly starving. For some reason, the new Supervisor picked on Jack a lot more than the others, and took great delight in keeping the brothers apart.

Last week, Jack had accidently bumped against the Matron in the corridor at breakfast time and he was dragged into the Supervisor's office where he was whipped with the horse whip kept in the cupboard. When Jack didn't cry out and beg for mercy, he was hit even harder, then thrown against the wall where he broke his arm. The Supervisor had then stormed out leaving him on the floor. Eventually, Jack managed to drag himself out of the office and was found by another boy who took him to Alfie.

Alfie had been planning to run away for a while and decided now was the time. He hid his brother in a laundry basket due to be collected that morning and hid in another, just before the laundry cart rumbled into the yard. Once outside the gates, when the cart stopped to pick up more laundry further along the road, Alfie quickly climbed out of his basket, helped Jack out of his and off the cart, then the boys ran and hid until it was dark.

They left town that night and walked into the country, sleeping under hay ricks or in barns, and eating whatever they could scrounge. They managed to hide on a variety of carts going along the road, which helped them get further from Lewes. Unfortunately, Jack's back and arm were getting more and more painful and they were forced to hide under the bush where Scruffy found them, and Jack couldn't move any further.

Dr Wilson arrived later in the morning and after checking Jack's back and changing the dressing, he asked Alfie to repeat his story. As one of the Workhouse board of guardians, he was stunned to hear of the recent treatment of the children by the new Supervisor and Matron. The reports sent to their meetings had been positive and there was no hint of mistreatment or starvation, though he had to admit they had not had a visit after the initial appointment, as a couple of planned visits had been postponed at the last minute. As the boys appeared happy to stay at the Hall, Dr Wilson was prepared to leave them in the Countess's care until he had investigated the accusations further.

During the following days, Jack's back slowly healed and he gradually regained his strength and desire to move downstairs and spend time in the kitchen with Mrs Smith. Alfie was often seen in the garden with Tom and Sam, helping them weed and dig the various flower and vegetable beds. Both boys were eating prodigiously and slowly gaining weight. Tess sent over a range of boy's clothing that had been stored in the attic, so both of the boys were warmly clad as the days became cooler.

Scruffy was friends with both boys and was often seen racing from the house to be with Alfie for a while, and then back to the house to be with Jack. He seemed quite relieved at meal times when they were both in the kitchen together.

Mary began to think about the boys' future as they settled into their new life at the Hall. She knew they were terrified at the thought of being sent back to the workhouse, but they were too young to be sent out to work. She was becoming very fond of the youngsters, who still slept in the room next to hers, and loved to have her tell them a story of bushrangers or farm life in Australia before being given a big hug and a kiss goodnight.

At one of the 'breakfast staff meetings', she told the staff she was thinking of applying to become their guardian. Everyone was very pleased as they too had become quite fond of the two lads. Polly said it was lovely to have youngsters in the Hall again, and both Joe and Robert welcomed them in the garden and the stables at any time. Mrs Smith was also enjoying Jack's company in the kitchen as he 'helped her with the cooking'!

Dr Wilson had spoken to his fellow Board of Guardians about Jack's beating and after some discreet investigation had brought to light the appalling treatment handed out to the children in the workhouse, the Supervisor and Matron were summarily sacked.

Mary had been asked to meet with the workhouse Board of Guardians, initially to give an account of finding the boys and of their behaviour during their stay at the Hall, and also to invite her to become member of the Board of Guardians. Her first reaction was to say no, but then she thought that maybe in her privileged position in the community, she might be able to bring about some changes for the better in the workhouse if on the Board.

Her request to be taken on a tour of the facility horrified many of the Guardians, but on her insistence, arrangements were made for all of them to be shown through the facility. Only Dr Wilson and one other

Guardian had actually seen inside the grim walls, and all were visibly shaken when they returned to the board room.

While they were still in a state of shock and calming their nerves with several glasses of brandy, Mary asked for, and was granted, access to the books and all financial paperwork. Mary's request to have permanent guardianship of Alfie and Jack was also quickly granted, much to her relief.

CHAPTER 17

Jack's wounds healed quickly and both boys were soon to be seen gallivanting around outside with Scruffy, or in the kitchen with Mrs Smith helping her to roll out pastry, or peel potatoes, which they knew would be rewarded with a scone or piece of cake. Both boys were devoted to Mary, who was enjoying their company in the huge Hall and beginning to look on them as she would two younger brothers. She realised, however, that if they were to grow up on the Estate, they would need to continue their education.

When discussing this with Celia, she was told that Sarah Green, the twenty-four-year-old daughter of an old friend of Mr Lyons, was seeking a new governess position. Sarah's father had been a Banker in the City of London and the family had lived in a large house in Notting Hill, employing a number of servants, in keeping with their upper class lifestyle. Sarah had attended a private ladies' college following her years at school, to learn the accomplishments such as music, sewing, and dancing required to equip young ladies for marriage.

Sadly, when Sarah was eighteen, both her parents had drowned when the ship they were sailing in struck rocks near the Isle of Wight. Regrettably for Sarah, it was discovered that her father had been renting the house and had been living way beyond his means, leaving Sarah in a precarious financial state with no home nor income.

Forced to seek work and lodgings, she applied for a live-in position as governess to a family with two young boys in Kent. Unfortunately, this position was terminated after five years when the boys were sent to boarding school.

Celia thought as well as being governess to Alfie and Jack, Sarah might be a good companion and mentor for Mary, who was desperately in need of developing social skills appropriate for her position.

Mary and Sarah were first introduced at a luncheon held by Celia, and the two young ladies spent the afternoon chatting in the garden. With only four year's difference in their ages, each recognised in the other someone they felt totally at ease with, and felt they could work together.

At first, the boys weren't at all pleased having to go up to the schoolroom each weekday to spend the morning learning to read and write. However, when Mary explained it was a condition of their being able to live at the Hall, they stopped complaining and settled down to their lessons.

Rather than become a live-in staff member, Sarah was offered— and accepted—one of the three cottages across the courtyard. The two-bedroom cottage had its own kitchen (to be supplied weekly with provisions from the Hall kitchen), a small sitting room, and bathroom. Sarah occasionally had dinner with the staff, but prepared her own breakfasts and lunches. This way she wasn't crowding the boys and had some independence in her off duty time.

Mary was beginning to understand that her title overrode existing social prejudices regarding her age and being a woman, and few men or women were prepared to dispute her decisions or requests. Such power, she realised, could easily be abused and was determined not to allow that to happen. She found Mr Lyons to be a great confidant who listened to her thoughts, and was prepared to offer her guidance when required.

Another person Mary was becoming very fond of was Tess Telford, who in her quiet, motherly way, recognised the lonely young lady still grieving for her lost mother while trying to cope with the enormous task landed so unexpectedly on her shoulders.

Mary would quite often ride Gem over to Home Farm early in the morning, with Scruffy loping along beside them. His legs seemed to be growing longer every day and he was starting to look rather like a shaggy greyhound. He and the farm dogs had developed an understanding to leave each other alone, but if at any time he felt threatened when Mary was inside, he would keep close to Gem.

Mary would sit and chat with Tess, or help her in the kitchen and some mornings, if early enough, would help with the milking. At first, the family were self-conscious in her presence but quickly relaxed when they saw the pleasure she gained by helping with jobs around the farm and in discussing the farm work with them.

Like Mr Lyons, Bob and Tess would listen to Mary's thoughts and plans and go through the pros and cons with her, reminding her not to buck the system too much too quickly.

CHAPTER 18

Early in July, Mary was stunned to receive an invitation from Buckingham Palace to attend a garden party Queen Victoria was holding at the end of the month, to meet new Peers of the Realm. Terrified at the prospect, Mary wanted to decline the invitation, but was promptly told one did not refuse an invitation to meet the Queen!

Every spare moment for the rest of the month was taken up with lessons on etiquette, how to address the Queen, appropriate responses to questions, etc., so much so that by the time Mary, Sarah, Celia and Mr Lyons travelled to London a week before the garden party, Mary's head was spinning. They stayed in the family residence in Mayfair, now staffed with a new butler, cook, and parlourmaid. Again, Mary couldn't believe the size of the residence, with so many rooms of all descriptions.

To take Mary's mind off her visit to the palace, Mr Lyons arranged for Mary to visit some of the businesses she owned and to meet the executives and senior staff. Celia and Sarah also took her out shopping, which didn't really do much to calm her nerves.

One night after dinner, Mary started a discussion on what should be done with the residence as she had no intention of spending more time in London than necessary. Sarah and Celia both tried to convince Mary that she would be expected to be in London for the season, but Mary was adamant that she would have nothing to do with it. She wasn't the least bit interested in spending any more time than was absolutely necessary socialising with the majority of the aristocracy she had met so far. She had found both the men and ladies to be incredibly self-centred, ostentatious and decadent. 'Empty-headed fops' was her opinion of them.

Adroitly shifting the conversation back to the fate of the residence, Mary spoke of her thoughts of the possibility of turning the building into a private hotel or boarding house. This caused some interesting debate that lasted well into the night and the next morning at breakfast. Finally, everyone agreed it might well be worth pursuing, much better than selling the building as Mary had intimated at one stage in their discussion. Mr Lyons said he would look into the feasibility of the plan, possible development costs, and expected return for the expenditure.

The day of the garden party dawned fine and sunny, much to Mary's relief. Mr Lyons escorted her to Buckingham Palace where she was met by a liveried footman who took her to a small reception room to wait, for what, she wasn't sure.

Imagine Mary's astonishment when the door opened not many minutes later and Queen Victoria walked in. Standing, Mary curtsied and greeted the monarch as she had been coached. Not sure what to do next, she waited for the Queen to sit and sat when gestured to do so. Queen Victoria told Mary she had known her grandmother well and was keen to meet her young granddaughter, now the Countess. She was very sad to hear how Lady Patricia had been treated by her brother and of her early death. She also said she had not realised how young Mary was to take on such a high ranking position with no training in the ways of the aristocracy, and was interested in hearing how she was coping.

Mary spent almost ten minutes talking alone with the Queen before a servant entered to say the other guests had arrived. To Mary's amazement, the Queen asked her to walk with her to the garden, saying she would be accepted more readily by her older peers if she was seen to enter with the Queen. It appeared the Queen had heard some derogative comments about Mary's age and colonial upbringing.

The rest of the afternoon passed in a blur for Mary, as she was introduced to many men and women, all of whom were extremely polite following Mary's entrance with the monarch. Mr Lyons was waiting at the palace gates to walk Mary back to the residence, where she spent the evening telling Celia and Sarah all about the afternoon.

Despite Mary's sudden favour with the aristocracy, who were now keen to be seen with her, she was relieved to leave the city and return to Longmire a couple of days after her visit to the palace.

Several of the local gentry, hearing of Mary's visit to Buckingham Palace, called at Longmire Hall to meet the young Colonial Countess, fully expecting her to be totally lacking in the social proficiencies expected of one of her status in their society. They were pleasantly surprised by her range of conversation, all be it in a strange accent, and her genuine interest in the local community.

Many had heard of her different approach to her servants and were amazed at Polly's and Jane's proficient dealing with all requests, whilst being respectful but not subservient. Both smiled while working and appeared to be enjoying their work, not usually condoned behaviour in servants.

Realising it was expected of her to entertain at times at Longmire Hall, Mary, Mrs Smith, and Polly set about planning some dinners for the local gentry. They decided four couples at a sitting would be a comfortable number to cater for at a time, having three dinners over a three-week period in August.

With the growing number of occupants in the Hall now eating meals in the servants hall, dinner was eaten in the breakfast room, with everyone seated around the larger table. They generally served themselves from dishes on the table or sideboard, but occasionally, these meals were used to help train all maids in the duties and skills required for serving at table. James was also given some training in the duties of preparing and serving wine at dinner.

Mary's neat, hand-written invitations sent to a variety of local gentry were accepted with alacrity. Those invited lived within easy carriage driving distance to allow for a safe drive home in the evening after dinner; as yet, Mary was not prepared to have strangers staying overnight at the Hall.

Mrs Smith was in her element, once again preparing to present a variety of courses for a number of guests like she used to when Mary's grandparents were both alive. Two extra village women were employed to help prepare the drawing and dining rooms, plus clean all the cutlery, silver and dinnerware.

Polly, Mary, and James ventured into the cellar to take stock of the wines stored there. Mary had little knowledge of wines but helped Polly and James list all the wine in the large underground cellar. Mr Lyons was a great help with suggestions of the types of wines that would be advisable to have on hand, and arranged for additional wines and spirits to be sent out to the Hall.

The first two dinners went without a hitch. As couples arrived, they were ushered into the drawing room and offered a sherry and hors d'oeuvres. At the appointed time, dinner was served and the guests thoroughly enjoyed the meal, and to their surprise, Mary's vivacious personality which led to lively conversation around the table.

Mary didn't like the way many of the so-called upper-class men treated their wives and daughters as chattels, assuming they were incapable of rational thought or conversation. So, at the dinner table she took great delight in discussing farming and business with the men, whilst also including the women in more general conversation, though at first they were rather hesitant to speak in front of the men.

Aware that at the end of a meal it was customary for the men to stay at the table to drink port with the host—while the women retired to the drawing room with the hostess—Mary decided to flout convention and asked all guests to withdraw to the sitting room. Her excuse was, as the hostess, she couldn't be in both rooms at the same time.

Before they withdrew, Mary thanked Polly, Jane, and James for their excellent service, which thrilled her staff and caused a few raised eyebrows from her guests. Mary knew how hard the three had tried to make the evenings run smoothly, and she was extremely proud of them.

CHAPTER 19

Regrettably, the third dinner didn't run as smoothly. Ronald Hawkins, a stout, surly, middle-aged man, arrived for dinner already under the influence of alcohol. He constantly belittled his younger wife in front of the other guests and was only just civil to Mary, much to the embarrassment of the others.

At the dining table, Ronald drank profusely, to the point where he became raucous, demanding more wine from James and trying to grab Jane when she was serving the dessert. Disgusted with this loutish behaviour, Mary announced that no more wine would be served as she didn't want any of the guests to become so inebriated that they wouldn't be able to appreciate Mrs Smith's excellent dessert. There was water on the table should anyone need further liquid refreshment.

When Ronald started to curse and swear at Mary, his wife begged him to be quiet. Turning to her, he punched her in the face so hard she was knocked sideways off her chair to lie in a crumpled heap on the floor.

Horrified, Mary demanded Ronald leave the room immediately. When he made no effort to rise, she walked to his chair and before he realised what she was about to do she grabbed the collar of his jacket and yanked him onto the floor. As he staggered to his feet, he swung his bunched fist at Mary's head, but was totally unprepared for her to duck and grab his fist, swinging him around and twisting his arm so far up his back he screamed in agony.

Quickly telling Polly to see to Mrs Hawkins, James to tell the Hawkin's groom to get his carriage to the front door as quickly as possible, and Jane to open the front door, Mary forced Ronald to stagger out into the hall, through the front door and down the front steps. There she gently propelled him forward as she let go of his arm and was pleased to see him lose his balance and sprawl on to the gravel drive.

Mary stood on the steps watching the poor groom try to drag his cursing employer into the carriage, and told Ronald he was no longer welcome on the Longmire Estate and that his wife would be taken home when she was fit to travel.

When Mary returned to the dining room, she found Jane had covered Mrs Hawkins with a blanket and was carefully bathing her bloodied face with water. Polly, in her absence, had asked the remaining guests to be seated and had given them all a small glass of brandy.

Kneeling beside Mrs Hawkins, who was beginning to regain consciousness, Mary thought her nose was possibly broken and her right eye was rapidly swelling shut. Assuring her that her husband had left and that she was welcome to stay the night, Mary asked James and one of her male guests to carry the poor woman up to the guest room and for Polly to put her to bed.

As no one felt like eating dessert, Mary took the remaining guests to the sitting room, offering further brandy or port to anyone who wished it. She began to apologise for the abrupt ending to the dinner, but was politely interrupted by one of her neighbours who said they applauded her actions, explaining that Ronald Hawkins had been throwing his weight around since his arrival in the district two years ago.

Requests to tone down his boorish behaviour had been rudely rejected and the men were astounded that a young woman had not only stood up to him, but had physically thrown him out.

As they left, all three couples said they were privileged to have Mary as their Countess and would be honoured if she would to visit their homes.

When everyone had driven down the drive, Mary went into the kitchen and collapsed into Mrs Smith's chair beside the fire. Handed a restorative mug of tea, Mary thanked all the staff for their efforts in what had turned out to be a very trying evening.

Polly was sitting beside Mrs Hawkins when Mary went upstairs to see her unexpected guest. Sobbing into a handkerchief, Lilly—as Mrs Hawkins asked them to call her—said she must get back home or her husband would kill her. Shocked at such a statement, Mary told her she should stay the night and wait till the doctor had seen her. Being quite late in the evening, Mary decided to send James to Lewes at daybreak to summon Doctor Wilson, and told her staff she would stay with Lilly throughout the night.

With Lilly tucked up in bed, wearing one of Mary's nightgowns, Mary listened to the sad tale of Lilly's forced marriage to Ronald Hawkins. Her father had owned a prosperous cutlery factory in Sheffield, South Yorkshire. Ronald had somehow worked his way into her father's favour and convinced him he would be a good husband for his only daughter.

Lilly had no say in the matter and found herself married at twenty to a brute of a man twenty-five years her senior. Six months later, in early 1884, Lilly's widowed father had died suddenly from a mysterious illness and Lilly inherited his fortune and factory. As a married woman, all of her inheritance belonged to Ronald and she had no access to any of it.

He immediately sold the factory and bought their current house— where she was kept more like a prisoner than his wife—regularly subjected to brutal beatings for the most minor transgression, and never allowed outside the Manor grounds. The only reason she had been allowed to accompany Ronald to Longmire that night was because the invitation was from the Countess.

Mary stayed with Lilly until just before dawn, when Polly brought up a cup of tea, telling her James had left to get the doctor. As Lilly had finally settled into a more relaxed sleep, Mary followed Polly down to the kitchen where she had a short nap in the chair beside the fire.

Doctor Wilson arrived just after breakfast and was shown up to the guest room where Lilly was slowly waking. He confirmed that Lilly's nose was broken and possibly her cheekbone as well, and declared she would need to stay in bed for at least a fortnight following such a blow to her head. He told Mary he would return the following day, better prepared to set Lilly's nose.

Outside the bedroom, he asked if Lilly could possibly stay at Longmire Hall as he didn't think she was fit to travel back to her home and was worried about the bruising he had seen on Lilly's back, arms, and legs. Mary confirmed that Lilly had told her that her husband regularly beat her, and told the doctor Lilly could stay at Longmire Hall for as long as was necessary.

That afternoon, Mary rode Gem into Lewes to speak to Mr Lyons about Lilly's situation. She was staggered to hear that not only did Ronald have total control of all Lilly's money, but also of Lilly herself. It was his right as a husband to keep her under control however he felt fit.

When Mary asked if he could be charged for the assault on Lilly the previous night, she was informed that not only would he not be charged but that he had the right to demand her immediate return to his house.

Furious at this callous treatment of a young woman, Mary told Mr Lyons she wanted Ronald Hawkins charged with assault on herself, explaining how he had tried to punch her and sworn at her in front of numerous witnesses.

Had Mary not been the Countess, Mr Lyons may not have taken Mary's accusation so seriously, but seeing her determination to follow it through, a clerk was sent for the police sergeant. Hearing her charge, he said he would go out to Mr Hawkins immediately—as a number of his workers had recently complained of his brutality—but he had been unable to charge the man without more proof.

Mary arrived back at the Longmire gate house just before sunset, to be warned by the gatekeeper that Mr Hawkins had just pushed his way through and ridden up to the hall. Forewarned, Mary took Gem in a roundabout way to the field behind the stables, leaving her to graze, while she ran to the back door.

A fact Mary had not made known since her arrival in England was that she carried her father's Colt.45 revolver in a discreet holster sewn into the pocket of her riding skirt whenever she went out riding. Polly was the only one who knew of the gun, as she had unpacked Mary's cases when she first arrived at Longmire Hall. She, however, didn't know that Mary was a crack shot, having been taught well by her father.

Slipping in through the back door, gun in hand, Mary could hear Ronald shouting at someone in the front hall to get his wife immediately. Entering the hall, she saw Ronald hit Jane across the shoulders with his riding whip then throw her to the ground. As he raised his foot to kick the poor girl, Mary shouted at him and Ronald whirled around to see who had called out.

Seeing Mary, he grinned, raised his whip, and strode towards her, only to pull up short when he saw the revolver pointing at him. Mary told him to turn around and go back outside, but after a moment's uncertainty, he proceeded towards her, telling her in the crudest fashion what he would do when he caught hold of her.

When he smirked and kept walking, disregarding her warning that she would shoot, she pulled the trigger, sending a bullet through his right knee. As he lay writhing on the floor clutching his leg, the Police sergeant and his constable ran through the front door. Bowing to Mary, the sergeant said he had heard Ronald's threats and her warning before she fired the gun as he ran up the front steps.

Once Ronald had been handcuffed and a sheet had been torn up to roughly bind his wound, the sergeant was fascinated to hold Mary's gun, as he had never seen a six-cylinder revolver before. Mary explained that her father had given her the gun after she had shown that she was very capable of handling such a weapon, whereas her brother Graham wouldn't even hold it.

CHAPTER 20

Lilly stayed at Longmire Hall for a month while her face healed, during which time her husband Ronald was held in custody until the next court of assize. When his day in court arrived, he was led into the court leaning on a crutch, looking very contrite when the charges were read out.

However, the moment Mary was called to give evidence, Ronald flew into a murderous rage, ranting and raving, screaming that he would kill her, then he turned his abuse on the Judge when he was called to order. When he refused to quieten down and stop struggling with the two constables who were trying to hold him, the Judge wasted no time in sentencing him to be confined in the Oxford County Pauper Lunatic Asylum.

Told to take the prisoner back to the cells, the constables began to drag the struggling man towards the stairs down to the cells. As they reached the top of the stairs, Ronald started to turn to shout further abuse at the Judge when his foot slipped off the top step and he pitched head first down the stairway. The horrified occupants in the courtroom were soon informed by a court official that the prisoner had died from a broken neck.

On Mr Lyons' advice, Lilly immediately applied for and was granted control of all of her husband's accounts and assets. While this was all being finalised, she moved into the empty cottage next to Sarah's at Longmire. Mary and Lilly had discussed this possibility before the trial, to give Lilly some security and company while her affairs were sorted out. Mary had also noted that Sarah and Lilly had become quite friendly, both being of the same age with similar social upbringing and interests.

Sarah's initial duties as lady's maid and social coach for Mary had been cut considerably as Mary developed her own way of dealing with her title. She had discovered that providing she was polite and not too radical, most people attributed her different approach to the way things were done to her colonial upbringing.

Mary didn't adhere to the practise of being dressed daily by her ladies maid. Only for the more formal occasions did Sarah assist her with dressing and 'dressing' her hair. Most days, Mary wore a long skirt, blouse and jacket if required, changing into her riding outfit when she went out on Gem. Consequently, Sarah had more time to herself and was pleased to have Lilly move into the cottage beside hers.

Both ladies, it turned, out were accomplished seamstresses. Lilly, while not actually being apprenticed to a well-known fashion house in Sheffield, had worked there for four years before her marriage. Mary bought them one of the new Singer sewing machines and employed both of them to make new staff uniforms, clothes for the boys, and Mary herself. They also took over the mending of linen as required. Both were very happy to be fully occupied, as well as having convivial company.

CHAPTER 21

The next rent day, which fell at the end of the week following Ronald's death, was a much different affair from the previous day Mary had observed. Mary had arranged with the Grey brothers and the butcher to have a lamb spitroast near the stables, and Mrs Smith prepared a vast array of salad dishes and cooked vegetables, so food was provided for all who could attend in the afternoon.

Mr Lyons assisted Mary collect the rent from each tenant, recording the amount and their signature or mark in the ledger. Tenants came and went with smiles on their faces, a far cry from the previous rent day.

A message had come through a few days before from Mary's other property, Oakdale in Yorkshire, enquiring when the Estate manager would be visiting. Mary had totally forgotten of its existence and felt bad that she had never visited them. She replied that she would visit Oakdale later in the month if it was convenient for the family.

During her frequent trips to the village, Mary had noticed two empty buildings next to the church hall. Tess Telford informed her that they had been the schoolhouse and village school until one day, Mr David for reasons unknown to anyone, had told Mr Morris to close the school and send the schoolteacher packing.

Before his death, David had taken over running the Estate for his mother who had little contact at that stage with anyone but David and the servants. As far as Tess knew, the Countess had no idea David was making such changes to the running of the Estate nor of his callous treatment of the tenants and servants.

Mary thought there would be about twenty village children, including Alfie and Jack, who would benefit from the reopening of the school, and asked Sarah if she would be interested in being the village teacher, with Lilly's assistance when required.

Keys for both buildings were found in the study desk and Mary was surprised to discover that the schoolroom was still furnished with all the desks, books, slates and stationary required to start teaching immediately. It appeared the door was locked when the teacher left, and nobody had been in there since. The small schoolhouse next door had also been left fully furnished when the teacher left.

Mary called a meeting of the families with children aged between five and fourteen, to tell them she would be reopening the school as soon as the school and school house had been thoroughly cleaned. Both boys and girls between the age of five and fourteen would be expected to attend.

She asked for women interested in earning some extra money by doing the cleaning to see her after the meeting, and also explained that all children who attended school would be given a free lunch. She explained that the food would be provided by the Estate, if the women could make up a roster for serving the food each school day. Women would also be fed on their rostered day on.

Despite the family rations being supplied by the Estate for the quarter, Mary was aware that more than half of the families struggled to have regular meals, as most of the men were poorly paid farm labourers. Consequently, the roster was filled very quickly.

The Estate owned all the buildings in the village, which consisted of the Church, vicarage and Church hall, the schoolroom and empty schoolhouse, plus residences and working facilities for the blacksmith and the wheelwright, the baker, butcher and grocer. The publican lived onsite at the local pub. The remaining dozen cottages were rented mainly by local farm labourers and their families. The buildings had become rundown through lack of maintenance and the majority of the tenants had started to lose the will to do anything but survive.

Now they had someone who not only had the money to make improvements, but was also prepared to listen to them and wanted to help and get them to take pride in their village once more. The villagers were getting used to their young Countess's regular visits to the village, and were constantly thankful for her desire to improve their lot in life;

a far cry from the past few years when they never saw or heard from the previous Countess, and were happy to see as little as possible of Mr David when he was managing the Estate.

They soon forgave Mary for sometimes bullying them into doing things for themselves, often finding a basket of groceries or something they needed at the back door when they had carried out the task required. No words said, just an acknowledgement that the job had been done.

CHAPTER 22

The next couple of weeks, Mary spent riding around the Estate checking on the barn repairs at Glendale, spending time on Farm two discussing prospective cattle sales and purchases with Matthew and John, and talking to Bob and Tess about her plans for the Estate and village.

Life was finally settling into a sort of routine between riding around the Estate, spending time with the boys, overseeing the preparations to open the school and spending time with the villagers. They enjoyed seeing their Countess wandering around the village, chatting to people and helping with odd jobs when needed. Some even overcame their initial embarrassment to invite Mary into their homes for a cup of tea.

Alfie and Jack were thrilled with the idea of going to school and playing with the village boys. Both boys were showing the benefits of regular healthy meals and plenty of exercise in the fresh air and sunshine. They loved being outside with Mary and Scruffy, and their biggest disappointment was not being able to go with Mary when she rode Gem around the Estate. Unbeknown to them, Mary and Robert were keeping a lookout for a couple of suitable ponies for the boys for Christmas.

Following a meeting with the Vicar's wife and the twins' mother to discuss the main issues besetting the village, Mary invited a small group of women to form a welfare committee. Their role was to let Mary know of villagers genuinely struggling to cope. At Mary's request, Dr Wilson or his assistant agreed to run regular fortnightly clinics in the church hall at rates subsidised by the Estate.

Once the boys went up to bed, Mary spent most of her evenings in the study doing the Estate bookwork. While she enjoyed doing this, she knew she should start looking for a suitable replacement for Mr Morris, although after discussions with Bob Telford and his son Will, she was starting to think she needed to employ someone who could also advise and assist the farmers on more modern farming techniques to increase the profitability of their farms.

During this time, Mr Lyons had been organising the trip to Yorkshire to visit the Oakdale Estate. He was going to accompany Mary as it would be a long, tedious journey with a number of train journeys and a couple of overnight stays before they arrived at the Estate. Also, he wanted to check on the contract with the incumbent Mr John Watson, who was actually managing the Estate, not leasing it as a tenant farmer.

Mary had written to the Watsons to give them the expected arrival time, and also to explain that she would be travelling as Lady Mary Evans—not using her full title—as she would like the visit to be as informal as possible, at least until she had met the family.

It was unfortunate that her visit to Yorkshire would clash with the planned opening of the school, but she felt sure Sarah—with Lilly's support—would cope admirably, so Mary told Sarah to start teaching when everything was ready. There didn't have to be a fancy opening ceremony before they could open the doors to the students.

Sarah and Lilly planned to move into the schoolhouse as soon as it had been thoroughly cleaned. Being next door to the school would give them more time to prepare for the expected students.

CHAPTER 23

Mary spent the night with the Lyons, prior to Mr Lyons accompanying her on the morning train to London. They stayed the night in a hotel, as the London residence was still being renovated, then caught the train to York early the next morning. Train travel was still a novel experience for Mary, but once she grew accustomed to the speed at which they were travelling, she thoroughly enjoyed the trip.

Mary was amazed at the change of scenery as they travelled north, again needing to adjust to the change of seasons in the northern hemisphere where it was now autumn and the trees' foliage were changing colour.

At York, they changed trains to Pocklington, which was the closest town to the Oakdale Estate. As it was late afternoon when they arrived in Pocklington, they booked into the Railway Inn for the night and sent a messenger to Oakdale to notify the Watsons of their arrival.

The next morning, as Mary was crossing the hotel foyer after breakfast, a tall, grey-haired gentleman mistook her for one of the hotel staff and asked if she could please bring him a pot of tea while he awaited his visitors' arrival.

Mary smiled and passed the message on to a maid, then went up to her room to prepare herself for the last leg of her journey. Imagine Mr Watson's embarrassment when ten minutes later, Mr Lyons introduced him to Mary. Smiling, Mary said she was pleased he had so readily embraced her request for informality!

John, as Mr Watson had asked them to call him, apologised that his wife Beth couldn't be with him to meet Mary and Mr Lyon. Their cook had sprained her ankle a few days ago and had gone to stay with her sister in a nearby village. Their daughter Angela, who was married to a Pocklington policeman, would normally have helped her mother but she had just had a baby, so Josie—their maid—had gone to look after the two other young children, to allow Beth to stay at home to be with her guests. Mary was concerned their visit would put too much pressure on Beth, but John assured them she would cope.

When Mary, Mr Lyons, and Mr Watson were aboard the waiting coach, the coachman set off on the half-hour journey to the Oakdale Estate. As they left Pocklington, Mary asked Mr Watson how long he had worked at Oakdale. He explained that his Grandfather had worked for Mary's Great Grandparents, and had been promoted to Manager when they left to live at Longmire Estate prior to the birth of their first child.

As far as Mr Watson was aware, Mary was the first member of the family to visit Oakdale since that day. His father had taken over as Manager when his father died, as had Mr Watson followed his father in the role. Due to this unbroken family succession and lack of connection with the Countess's family, few—if any—of the local people knew that Mr Watson was the Manager, and not the owner of Oakdale Estate, which was by far the largest land holding in the district.

His father had been called Squire and the name had passed to him when he took over. He assured Mary he took the token title seriously and was heavily involved in the local community, helping the needy when possible. Profits from the Estate were kept in an account to be used for the upkeep of the Estate, and also for some community support.

He told them he and his wife Beth also had two sons. Paul was twenty-six, and lived with them on the Estate. He worked with his father and hoped to take over the management of the Estate when his father retired. Hugh, the younger son, was twenty-one and had just completed his studies at the Royal Agricultural College in Gloucestershire, and was expected home in a few days.

Soon the coach passed through an imposing set of gates with Mary's crest on each gate post. A large country manor house stood at the end of a long avenue of large oak trees. As they drew closer, Mary saw a rambling, grey stone, double storied house covered in ivy, with a flat roof surrounded by a stone balustrade. The front door was covered by a portico to protect passengers at the doorway from the Yorkshire weather.

A small, grey-haired lady stood in the open doorway beside a tall young man with brown curly hair, as the coach pulled up. When John handed Mary down from the coach, the lady glanced at her, then stood looking towards the coach until John called her to get her attention. Like John, Beth had been expecting to meet an older woman, possibly dressed in the fine travelling clothes often worn by those flaunting their position.

Following John's introduction, Beth was about to curtsey when Mary took her hand and told her how nice it was to meet her, and to please call her 'Mary'. The young man introduced himself as Paul, and then greeted Mr Lyons who had alighted from the coach and was being introduced.

As John led the way inside to the sitting room, Beth excused herself to get the tea and scones she had prepared. While Mary and Mr Lyons were chatting to Paul, John left the room to help his wife wheel in the trolley. While in the kitchen, he reminded Beth of Mary's desire to be as informal as possible and reassured her that Mary had not come to dismiss them

A far more cheerful Beth entered the sitting room, and was soon telling Mary of their new grandson who was only two weeks old. Mary was happy to see her relax as she chatted, and was pleased when Beth accepted her offer of assistance to take the trolley back to the kitchen.

She assured Beth that she actually felt more comfortable in the kitchen than in the more formal rooms, and explained a little of how she and her staff ran Longmire Hall. She also said John had explained about their lack of staff and expressed the hope that she might be treated as one of the family to save the extra work guests created. She was sure Mr Lyons, who was only staying the night, would agree.

So, soon after Mr Lyons and Mary had been shown to their rooms, Mr Lyons and John retired to the Estate office to go through the Estate books, and Mary helped Beth prepare lunch.

After lunch, Beth told Mary she had a roast ready to put on for dinner and asked if Mary would like to go for a ride with Paul. Mary thought this was a wonderful idea, after sitting in coaches and train carriages for so long, and went up to her room to change into her riding outfit.

Paul was surprised, but somewhat relieved, when Mary told him she rode astride. They still had his mother's side-saddle, but her horse was quite elderly now and hadn't been ridden for years.

Mounted on a striking bay mare, Mary spent a wonderful couple of hours riding through the fields where Shorthorn cattle were grazing, and going through copses of various types of trees, mostly bare of leaves. Many of the fields were also bare, and Paul explained they grew various crops that were harvested to feed the cattle in the barns.

Back at the house, Mary spent time with Mr Lyons when Paul and his father left to milk the cows. He told her John kept the books well, both for the Estate and his personal income and costs. However, he told her there were some things he would need to discuss with her when they had more time in the morning.

The following morning, after a large hot breakfast in the cosy country kitchen, Mr Lyons and Mary retired to the Estate office while John and Paul went out to clean the cow barn. As Mr Lyons went through the books with Mary, she realised the Estate was a very profitable property, while the Watsons appeared to be only just making ends meet.

When she queried Mr Lyons about this, he said John had told him that Mr Morris had made sweeping changes to his contract when he called early the previous year. Mr Morris had told them that he was increasing the percentage of any profit to go to the Countess's account, plus he informed John the estate would no longer pay wages for the cook, maid, nor the dairymaid, who made the butter and cheese sold each week. He said, as their children were grown up, Beth could carry out those jobs.

Two of the estate workers were dismissed, Mr Morris insisting that John and his two sons should be able to cope. He wouldn't even consider John putting Paul on the payroll, and told John his contract would be revoked if he argued. John had been using his savings to pay the cook and maid to help Beth, who spent many unpaid hours in the dairy, and he also paid Paul a small wage. They had not seen Mr Morris since that visit and had no knowledge of his downfall.

When Mary saw the small amount John withdrew as wages from the estate per month, she raised her eyebrows at Mr Lyons and asked what would be a fair wage for a manager of a large estate with a number of employees on the payroll. He replied that John was being severely underpaid, his wage seemingly not having changed much from his father's thirty years ago. To be expected to pay the estate employees as well was absurd. Knowing what they did of Mr Morris's greedy, uncaring dealings at Longmire, neither Mary nor Mr Lyons was surprised to see what he had demanded at Oakdale.

For the rest of the morning, they worked on a new contract for the estate manager and his son, plus reinstated the cook, maid, and dairymaid to the payroll. A smaller percentage of the profits was allotted to Mary's account, the remainder to be used for Estate maintenance and community assistance.

Mary wondered where Mr Morris had banked the additional percentage he had removed from the Estate account, and where the books for Oakdale had been kept. Mr Lyons suggested they go to the bank in Pocklington that afternoon to check, and also to have Mary's name put on the estate account. He was catching the late afternoon train to York as he couldn't stay away from his office for too long.

John accompanied them to Pocklington and introduced Mary to the Bank Manager, using her full title with her permission. They quickly completed the Estate account paperwork, and cancelled Mr Morris's authority to withdraw funds from the Estate. Mr Lyons gave a brief account of Mr Morris's fraudulent dealings and consequent imprisonment, then asked if he had an account in his own name at the bank. The manager told them he did have an account, and added that he also had a safety deposit box. They couldn't access the accounts or deposit box, but the Bank Manager told Mary she would be able to see both as soon as she produced a signed order from the Judge who had presided over Mr Morris's court case and sentencing.

Mary was determined to find out if the bank held more of Mr Morris's embezzled money, so she decided to extend her stay in Yorkshire to give Mr Lyons time to send up the relevant information. She asked him to send a message to Longmire Hall to let them know she would be away longer than planned.

CHAPTER 24

After seeing Mr Lyons on his way to York, Mary and John walked back to the hotel, as it was considered not safe to travel back to the estate in the dark. As they walked into the hotel foyer, a young man, who looked remarkably like John, greeted him with an enthusiastic hug, asking his father why he was in town.

Disentangling himself from the embrace, John introduced his younger son, Hugh, to a rather startled Mary, and then suggested they all go into the dining room for dinner. As they waited for their meal, Hugh explained that he had just arrived in Pocklington and had planned to stay the night at the hotel before hiring a horse in the morning to ride home to Oakdale.

At first, Hugh found it hard to believe that Mary could be a Peer of the Realm, as she had none of the airs and graces that put him off the daughters of the aristocracy he was forced to mingle with at social functions near his College. Also, she was younger than he was and seemed just like a friendly country girl with a funny accent.

On their return to Oakdale the next morning, Mary told John and Beth of the proposed changes to his contract and Estate staffing, and running costs. They were speechless at first, then thanked Mary profusely. To allow the family time to discuss their new circumstances, Mary excused herself and went for a walk in the garden.

Ten minutes later, Hugh found her sitting on a bench with one of the farm cats curled up on her lap. After thanking her again for what she was arranging for his family's future, he asked her if she would be interested in accompanying him while he checked the cows in the barn, and the pigs in their enclosure. As they walked, Hugh explained their pigs spent the nights in their pens, but free-ranged in selected fields during the days, except when the snow became too deep.

Mary was intrigued to see the large red-and-white cows that Hugh told her were Ayrshire cows, all tied in separate stalls in the barns, placidly eating from feed bins in front of them. She told him she had lived on a dairy farm in Australia where they milked the smaller Jersey cows that spent day and night all year round out in the paddocks eating grass, only coming to the shed to be milked. Mary and Hugh spent the rest of the morning discussing their shared interest in farming. Mary wanted to hear more about Hugh's Agricultural studies, while he was fascinated to hear of her own farming experiences.

After lunch, Mary spent time with John and Paul, explaining in more detail the new contract Mr Lyons would be drawing up for John, including Paul as assistant manager. She also told them that all the workers, both inside and out, would have their wages increased to be on par with those at Longmire Estate down south. Beth would also be recompensed for the long hours she had worked in the dairy over the past year, producing the butter and cheese sold for the Estate.

John confided in Mary that he was worried about Beth's health. Usually an energetic, cheerful person, she had become withdrawn and lethargic. Mary wondered if the combination of the additional work in the dairy and house, combined with the worry about their financial situation, might have led to these changes.

Mrs Turner, the cook, was due back the following morning and Mary suggested that John try to convince Beth to spend some time with her daughter and grandchildren. Maybe not exactly the rest she needed, but a break from her normal work. Emma, the maid, could return to Oakdale and Mary said she would love to help where possible.

At first John was reluctant to even consider the proposition, with Mary staying as a guest. But, as she explained, her visit had been extended to wait for the letter for the bank manager. Mary added that she would find it very hard to sit around being 'a lady' all day so he relented and went to speak to his wife.

The next morning, Paul set off to Pocklington, with Beth sitting on the carriage seat beside him, not looking happy at leaving such a titled guest, but accepting it had to be so. Paul would bring Emma back with him and would also collect Mrs Turner from her sister's, so Beth thought Mary wouldn't have much to do.

Little did she know that Mary and Hugh would take over the butter and cheese making before a new dairy maid was employed, and that Mary would also help with the milking and other jobs around the farm. She found the Ayrshires with the longer teats easier to milk than the Jerseys she had milked at home, and was often in the barn at dawn to assist with the morning milking.

Some afternoons, she and Hugh would ride around the Estate and he told her more about his studies in Agriculture. During the evenings after dinner, Mary was quite happy to sit back and listen to Hugh discussing with his father and brother how they could increase the productivity of their pastures and crops, and improve the breeding of their cattle.

As she listened, the gem of an idea started to form. Although only twenty-one, Hugh would be an ideal Estate Supervisor, a combination of the Estate Agent, plus someone to assist the tenant farmers modernise their farming techniques and increase their profitability. When Mary discussed the idea with Hugh, he was very keen to have a go, especially when Mary said his duties would be spread between both Estates. That would mean he could spend some of the year at home helping his father and brother.

When Mary asked him when he would be able to start, Hugh told her all graduating students at the College were expected to remain on site for at least two weeks after Graduation Day, which was in just over a month on the twenty third of November. So he thought it would be close to the middle of December before he could get to Longmire Estate.

John and Paul were very pleased to hear of Hugh's possible employment, especially when they heard he would be working at Oakdale too. John had thought a lot about his younger son's evening discussions, but had wondered just how much the Estate could afford to put into practice. Now he had Mary's approval without having to ask her!

Just over a week after Mr Lyon's return to Lewes, a letter arrived from the Judge, stating that the Court's ruling would apply to Mr Morris's bank accounts and safety deposit box at the Pocklington bank. He gave permission for Lady Mary to have access to both the account and safety deposit box, before the bank arranged to have the money transferred to her Lewes account.

John and Hugh travelled to Pocklington with Mary, where she found the safety deposit box key from Mr Morris's key ring, that the Judge had included with the letter, opened the deposit box. Inside were two small ledgers, an amount of cash, and a gold hunter watch that John said had belonged to his grandfather. The watch had gone missing, with some cash at about the time of Mr Morris's last visit, but they hadn't considered he might have stolen it.

As at Longmire Estate, one ledger had the amount John had signed for, with the increase to the amount to go into the Countess's account, and the second with the original amount with a very good forgery of John's signature. The bank account had one entry for the amount of the alleged additional profit.

With the contents of the deposit box in her bag, Mary, John and Hugh went to Amanda's house to collect Beth, who was ready to go home. Mary met Amanda's husband, Peter—who was just heading off to work—looking resplendent in his uniform. John told him of finding his watch and money in the deposit box, and Mary explained that Mr Morris was already in prison.

Now that the bank issue had been sorted, Mary felt she should be returning to Longmire. Hugh had to return to the College at Cirencester in Gloucestershire in a few days, so it was decided that he would accompany her to London, and then head off to the College.

When they arrived in London the following afternoon, Mary was surprised at how sad she felt as she watched Hugh stride off to catch the train for Cirencester, knowing she wouldn't see him again for over two months. With a heavy heart, she followed the porter to the cabstand where he loaded her luggage, and gave instructions for her to be taken to the hotel where she had stayed previously.

CHAPTER 25

Two days later, as Mary walked through Hyde Park on her way back to the hotel, after lunch with some of her factory managers, she noticed a small girl huddled on a bench near the gate. She was dressed in a thin cotton dress, shivering violently in the cold wind, and appeared to be sobbing. When Mary approached her, she started then tried to curl up into a smaller shape and hide behind the branches of an overhanging shrub.

Before Mary could speak, another small girl raced through the gate and sat on the bench, grabbing the other girl and hugging her tightly, murmuring soothing words to her. While doing this, she glared at Mary, as if daring her to interfere.

Speaking quietly, Mary asked if she could please rest her tired legs by sitting at the end of the bench, and was answered by a brief nod from the second girl. As she sat on the bench, Mary glanced at the girls, noting that they appeared quite young and looked very alike.

She told them her name was Mary and chatted about her morning in the city. As the girls appeared to relax, she asked their names and was hesitantly told they were Sally and Jane Martin. When asked where they lived, she was told they didn't have a home and slept anywhere they could find shelter.

Shocked at this response and becoming worried about the shivering of both girls, she asked them if they would like to go with her to the hotel to warm up and have something to eat before it became dark. As they walked beside her, the two girls clung to each other and it became apparent that Sally, the first girl she had seen, was blind.

Gently encouraging the girls to accompany her up the steps into the foyer of the hotel, Mary asked the doorman to request that the housekeeper meet her in her rooms as quickly as possible, and then she led the girls up the stairs to her suite on the first floor.

The housekeeper arrived as Mary was settling both girls in front of the fire in her sitting room. She quickly explained how she had found the girls, and asked if she could please have a maid sent up to assist her bathe and feed the girls, and also to be a witness that she was not accosting or kidnapping the girls. Mary also requested a visit from the hotel doctor, and the name of a local law firm she could contact in the morning. She also asked to meet with the hotel detective to explain what was happening.

A young woman called Meg, arrived soon after the housekeeper left, carrying a tray with two glasses of warm milk and some bread and jam. While Meg ran the bath, Mary encouraged the girls to eat the bread and drink the milk. After an initial hesitation, they both devoured the food very quickly—Jane assisting Sally with the glass of milk and handing her the food.

Neither girl was at all keen to get into the bath, but once they were soaking together in the warm water after their hair had been washed, it was hard to entice them to get out. Eventually, each girl was wrapped in a warm, fluffy towel, and again in front of the sitting room fire.

Mary was intrigued to see Sally constantly stroking her towel and rubbing it on her cheek. Jane noticed her watching Sally, and explained that the fluffy towel felt like a toy bear Sally used to love stroking and cuddling. Unfortunately, the bear had been left behind when they had to leave their house when their Grandmother died.

Although she would have dearly loved to find out more about the girls, Mary could see they were getting very sleepy, so she and Meg dressed them in a couple of Mary's work shirts and put them to bed in the maid's room next to Mary's bedroom. Mary assured them that she would stay in the suite while they slept, and Meg said she would sleep on the couch in the room with the girls.

The next morning, after a breakfast of porridge, toast and milk, the doctor arrived and checked both girls, announcing them to be surprisingly healthy for the life they had recently been living. He gave Mary the address of a nearby lawyer, and wrote a note of introduction for her before he left.

Both girls seemed more relaxed with Mary and Meg in the morning, and were more prepared to tell their story. Jane was very protective of Sally, assisting her with most activities and she was also the main speaker. She told them she and Sally were eight-year-old twins who had lived in Hoxton with their mother, after their father had been killed at work. Their mother had been knocked down and killed by a runaway horse and cart a year later. Sally had been with her mother and had been knocked unconscious, but had appeared to be uninjured. However, when she woke up in the hospital, she couldn't see.

Their grandmother, who lived near the river, had taken them in and they had lived there about a year until she died suddenly a few weeks ago. They had no idea if they had any other relatives. The next-door neighbour had taken the girls in when the landlord had immediately rented the house to another family, but her husband insisted the girls be sent to the workhouse.

Hearing this, Jane and Sally had run away and lived on the streets until Mary had found them in the park. Jane was terrified she and her sister would be separated, as she had heard that Sally's blindness would mean she would be sent to a different place. Mary knew from her work on the Board that workhouses didn't like having disabled people thrust upon them, and tried hard to segregate them from the other inmates. As a blind eight-year-old girl, separated from her twin, Sally's life would be a nightmare if she was put in the workhouse.

Before she met the lawyer, Mary asked the girls if they would like to visit her home in the country while a suitable place was found where both girls could stay together. Jane replied that they would like to stay with Mary, especially if Meg could go too, as Sally felt very comfortable with the maid.

When Mary took Jane aside and asked if she minded Meg taking over some of the responsibility dealing with Sally's needs, Jane replied that though she loved her sister dearly and took looking after her very seriously, she was thrilled as it would allow her to have some time to herself.

Mary spoke to the housekeeper and Meg about the possibility of Meg travelling to Longmire Estate with the girls. Meg was excited at the idea of leaving London and spending some time in the country, and the housekeeper said she could have unpaid leave from the hotel to assist Lady Mary.

Mary left the girls in the hotel suite with Meg while she went to see the lawyer mid-morning, promising to take them shopping for some warmer clothes and boots when she returned.

Mr Brown, the lawyer, was a middle-aged gentleman with steel-rimmed glasses, who reminded Mary of a sleepy owl as he sat behind his desk, blinking often as he turned his head regularly to look out the window, and then back at Mary. After reading the doctor's letter, he said he could see no reason why Mary couldn't look after the girls if she so desired. He seemed to be more interested in having a Countess in his office than the girls' future. Mary had to ask him a couple of times if he would undertake a search for possible relatives. Eventually, by the time she left the office, Mary had an agreement from Mr Brown to carry out an investigation on her behalf.

After a quick lunch on her return to the hotel, Mary asked reception to book tickets for the four of them on the following days' early train to Lewes, and then the four of them set off shopping. Meg suggested they go to the market to look for suitable clothing for the girls after Mary said she wanted serviceable clothes—not fancy, frilly dresses from the nearby shops.

At a stall run by a distant relative of Meg's, they found several pinafore dresses of suitable size and warm material, so Mary gave the girls the choice of picking three dresses each. She was touched at the way Jane held each dress up for Sally to hold and explained the colour and style, before choosing her own. Each girl was also fitted with a woollen coat and several articles of underwear and nightwear, before they left to buy some boots.

Mary was determined to have the girls fitted with good quality boots, so they set off down the street for the shoe shop. On the way, they passed a shop with some dolls displayed in the window and on a whim Mary led the way into the shop. Looking around, there were many different dolls, plus many types of toys, and in an area near the counter, teddy bears of all sizes.

As Meg walked ahead with Sally holding her hand, Mary asked Jane if there were any teddy bears similar to the one Sally had been so attached to. She pointed to a furry yellow bear, so Mary picked it out and asked Jane if she would like to give it to her sister. The canny young lass shook her head and whispered it would be better if Meg gave it to her.

When Meg handed the bear to Sally, the look of surprise on her face was quickly lost as the bear was clutched to her chest and her face was buried into its fur. Muffled words were heard as the young girl talked lovingly to the soft toy.

Hearing a faint sigh from Jane, Mary asked her if she had a favourite toy when they were with their grandmother. Jane nodded and pointed to a rag doll sitting to the side of all the fancily-dressed porcelain dolls. Mary walked over to the shelf and carefully picked up the doll, and handed it to Jane who burst into tears as she hugged it. When an astounded Mary asked what the matter was, Jane said she was crying because she was so happy!

Finally, they arrived at the boot store where Mary asked for the girls to be fitted for some sturdy boots, shoes, and slippers. Using her title this time, the attendants took great care to pick footwear that were soft and comfortable. Both Mary and Meg had to cover their smiles at the look of bliss on both girls' faces as their feet were buttoned into their new boots. Apparently, they had always had second-hand footwear that didn't always fit properly.

Dinner back at the hotel was a joyful affair, both girls clutching their new cuddly toy. The girls were keen to go to bed early after the hectic afternoon's shopping, which left Mary and Meg free to pack their cases. Mary had bought a small case for each of the girls, and had also bought Meg a warm woollen shawl and some boots more suitable for country use. Meg left for a while to pack her own belongings, and to say goodbye to her friends on the staff.

CHAPTER 26

At first, the girls were scared when the train pulled out of the station the next morning, but soon settled to enjoy the journey to Lewes. Jane and Meg spent a lot of the time describing the scenery to Sally, which allowed Mary time to sit back and think about her trip up North and also her return to Longmire Hall.

Celia Lyons was waiting to greet them at Lewes station, having received a telegraph message of their expected arrival time. She took them home and after a quick lunch, the girls were very happy to have an afternoon sleep. That night, the twins were introduced to Mr Lyons at dinner time and Mary was thrilled to see both girls using manners they had obviously been taught earlier in their short lives.

It was decided to spend the next day in Lewes before introducing the girls to all the people at Longmire Hall, so a message was sent for Robert and James to bring the coach and cart the following day.

In the morning, while Meg and Celia took the twins for a walk in the local park carrying a bag of bread crusts to feed the ducks, Mary visited Mr Lyons in his office to discuss her trip to Oakdale and also to explain her concern for the girls' future.

Early the next morning, Mary was awoken by two very excited girls who were ready to set off for Longmire straight away, even though it was still dark. Finally, they were convinced it was too dark for the horses to travel safely, and climbed into bed with Mary for a cuddle before breakfast. When Meg came in later with a cup of tea for Mary, she found all three sound asleep.

With breakfast finally eaten, the girls went out to the front garden to await the arrival of Mary's coach. Although young, the girls had some idea of Mary's title, though what it actually entailed was somewhat blended with fact and fiction. By the time Robert and James arrived at the front gate, the girls had convinced each other the coach would be golden and the coachman would be in full regalia. Somewhat to their disappointment, neither was the case, but they quickly regained their excitement when Robert sat them on the seat beside him while James went to the house to announce their arrival.

Finally, with the luggage in the carriage, Mary and Meg in the coach, and the twins wrapped in a thick travelling rug sitting beside Robert, they set off for Longmire. The girls had wanted to travel all the way on the driver's seat, but a compromise had been struck by Robert, who said they could travel through the town with him, but would have to travel in the coach when they left the town. So the remainder of the trip was spent in the coach with Meg and Jane chatting to Sally, explaining what they were travelling past. Mary sat back and watched Meg dealing with the girls, amazed at the way she spoke and dealt with Sally as though she could see.

Of course, she guided her when necessary but never made a fuss about it. Mary had noticed that when Meg walked with Sally, she was encouraging her to put her hand on Meg's arm, rather than Meg holding her as they walked. If she wanted to hold hands, that was allowed, but she wasn't pulled along as often happened when blind people were being assisted. Meg had also started to encourage Sally to use a spoon to feed herself—rather than waiting to be spoon-fed all the time—and was teaching her to use a cup by herself.

The staff, Alfie, and Jack were all waiting on the front steps when the coach came down the drive to Longmire Hall, and cheered as it pulled up in front of them. Although she had only been in England for four months and had been away from Longmire Hall for three weeks, this felt like a great homecoming. The staff were thrilled to see her home safely and were intrigued to see the twins in the coach.

As Mary stepped down from the coach, she was knocked to the ground by Scruffy, who had launched himself from the top step and landed in her arms. As she unsuccessfully tried to stop the excited hound licking her face, Robert jumped from the coach, wrapped his arms around the excited dog and hauled him off Mary.

Laughing, she stood up and dusted herself off before greeting the quivering dog rolling at her feet, and then the staff and boys waiting on the steps. Once greetings were over, Mary asked them all to go to the sitting room where she would introduce her visitors.

Robert restrained Scruffy, who would have loved to greet each girl with a lick, as Meg and the girls followed Mary up the steps and into the hall. As Jane gazed around the huge entrance, Meg quietly explained what she saw to Sally. Like the twins, Meg was aware of Mary's title and was slowly relaxing and trying hard to follow her request to treat her in a less formal manner, especially when they were not in public. However, she was not prepared for the informal manner in which the staff greeted Mary, laughing when Scruffy knocked her over, and each giving her a welcoming hug as she walked up the steps.

When they were all together in the sitting room, Mary introduced each member of the staff to Meg and the girls, explaining that for the moment, the girls were holidaying at the Estate and Meg was their maid. Jack and Alfie each gave Mary a big hug then stood back, and watched the two young girls being greeted by the staff. Mary knew she would have to quickly allay their fears that their place in the household would be usurped.

As the staff dispersed, Mary asked Polly to arrange for the spare bedroom with an attached maid's room to be prepared for the girls and Meg. Like Mary, Meg had noticed the boy's wary greeting to the girls, so she suggested she would take the girls up to help prepare their room to give Mary time alone with Alfie and Jack, who had been given the day off school to welcome her home.

Sitting together in front of the fire, Mary asked the boys what they had been doing in her absence. Quickly, they forgot about the girls and excitedly told Mary all about their days at school, which had started over a week ago. They also told her of the work they had been doing at home. Jack had been helping Mrs Smith in the kitchen and proudly announced he had cooked the pie they were to have for dessert that night. Not to be outdone, Alfie said he had helped Tom grow the vegetables, and he had picked them all by himself.

Congratulating them both on their endeavours, Mary explained why the girls were visiting and assured the boys that they were very much part of her family and would stay that way, no matter who else came to visit or stay. She added that she hoped they would make the girls feel welcome, and explained about Sally not being able to see.

The boys wanted to know if the girls would be attending school with them while they were staying at the Hall. Not sure of the girls' future, Mary hadn't thought about their immediate education, but said she would talk to Sarah before making a decision.

CHAPTER 27

Thrilled to be home again, Mary spent time chatting to all her staff, and also visited all three farms, revelling being on Gem's back again. Scruffy was in his element loping along beside them wherever they went. Mary had asked the boys to show Jane, Sally and Meg around the grounds, gardens, and the stables while she was visiting the farms. Jane had a wonderful time chatting to the boys while Sally was happy to have Meg's sole attention as they followed slowly behind the other three.

The next day, Mary walked to the village to meet Sarah and Lilly who proudly showed her through the school. She was thrilled to hear how enthusiastically the villagers had supported the opening of the school, and how keen the ten girls and eight boys were to attend. The meal roster was working well, with plans to provide hot soup as the weather became colder. Sarah and Lilly had moved into the schoolhouse and had offered the use of their kitchen to cook the soup and possibly, some stews later on.

Before her return to the Hall, Mary told Sarah about Jane and Sally, and asked what she thought about them attending school while staying at the Estate. Sarah could see no reason why Jane shouldn't attend, but was unsure how Sally would cope. Mary decided to discuss this with Meg before she made a decision about either girl's attendance.

When the children were in bed, Mary and Meg sat in front of the fire in the study to discuss the girl's education. Like Sarah, Meg felt Jane would benefit from attending school but thought Sally would be better off staying with her where she could teach her. Sally was already showing great aptitude in developing new skills as Meg showed her ways to cope with her blindness. She was starting to feed herself, was dressing herself in clothes put out for her, and was also much more confident walking around with her hand on Meg's arm rather than clinging to her guide.

The next morning, Mary, her staff, Meg, and the four children walked to church, the girls revealing that they had never been to church before. Both girls loved the singing and sat quietly throughout the rest of the service. Sally coped quite well with the number of people coming up to Mary after the service to welcome her back, and she and Jane walked back to the Hall arm in arm humming the hymns they had heard.

Before dinner, Mary and Meg took the girls into the study to have a talk about school. Jane said she would love to go but knew Sally wouldn't cope, so she would stay home too. However, Sally told her not to be silly, they would still be together after school and she needed to learn more from Meg.

Mary found it hard to believe that the twins were only eight years old when she heard them talking in such a matter of fact way. Sally realised her dependence on Jane was stopping her sister from doing things she liked to do, while Jane was fiercely protective of her sister and had, for the past two years, unselfishly done everything for Sally.

So the next morning, Alfie and Jack took Jane to school with them after Mary had asked them to help her settle in. Both boys were loving school and were happy to take Jane with them. Mary had gone to the school earlier to be there to introduce Jane to Sarah, and then she left to wander through the village, chatting to the villagers she met, and catching up on news from the past three weeks.

Back at the Hall, Sally and Meg were at the stables where Robert was introducing them to the horses, speaking quietly as he carried Sally to the stable door where Rusty stretched out his head to be patted. Sally laughed when he blew hot air on her cheek and loved the feel of his soft lips when he gently took the sugar Robert had placed on her palm.

Asked if she would like to sit on his back, Sally agreed providing Meg held her hand; so Rusty was led out of the stable and Sally was placed on his back. Her right hand was placed on his mane and she was told to hang onto the hair when he moved forward. Meg walked beside Rusty, holding Sally's left had as Robert slowly led Rusty around the courtyard; he was pleased to see Sally's big smile as they moved around.

As they were about to leave the stables, Meg noticed the lunging whips hanging on the tack room wall, which reminded her of the thin cane her cousin had used to help him walk unassisted. She asked Robert if there might be whip handles that could be used as a walking cane for Sally, explaining how it would be used extended in front of her to detect objects before she tripped over them, not as a walking stick. He told her he would see what he could find.

That evening, before the evening meal, Robert presented Sally with a whip handle cut down to reach a little above her waist. It had a loop to put around her wrist and also a small knob on the end to stop it being a dangerous point. After thanking him, Meg explained to Sally that she would start to teach her how to use the cane in the morning. This gift from Robert helped Sally cope with Jane's obvious excitement about her first day at school, the first time the girls had spent a day apart experiencing different activities.

During the next few weeks, the girls settled into the life of theHall, the boys happy to accept them into their adopted family. After school, Jane and the boys would race into the kitchen for a glass of milk and a slice of Mrs Smith's cake. Sally would meet them there and she and Jane would discuss their day's activities. If the weather was too cold or wet, Jane and the boys were taken to and collected from school in a covered cart driven by James, with Sally sitting beside him on the driver's seat.

The young blind girl was quickly becoming a favourite with the staff, who were impressed with her uncomplaining efforts to cope with her disability. Often they would stop to chat to her, explaining what they were doing and sometimes allowing her help them polish a table or help make some scones.

CHAPTER 28

In the third week following her arrival home, Mary received a letter from the lawyer Mr Brown, saying his investigation had turned up a distant relative of the girls, who was interested giving the girls a home. Little more was said other than a request for further instructions on how Mary wanted this to progress.

Not at all happy with what the letter told her, or more so what was not revealed about this distant relative, Mary drove herself into Lewes to speak to Mr Lyons. After reading the letter, he agreed with Mary that there was a lot more information required before the girls would be moved, then told her he had a friend who was a Private Detective living in Kensington who dealt with cases such as this. Immediately, he wrote a note to his friend, while Ben made a copy of Mr Brown's letter to be included with the note and then sent Ben out to post the letter.

Early in November, Mr Lyons arrived at Longmire Hall accompanied by his friend Richard Smyth, the Private Detective. After lunch, Richard told Mary that he had used the information Mr Brown gave him to track down Hester Martin, who claimed to be a relative of the twins. Before they met face to face, he sourced information from local people who knew Hester, but found few people who had a good word to say about her. The local constabulary told him Hester was suspected of being involved in several thefts in the area and also of entertaining gentlemen in her apartment to supplement her income.

Richard said he followed Hester from her address in a squalid alley in Whitechapel to a nearby public house, where he watched her drink gin steadily for a couple of hours, bragging to anyone who would listen that soon she wouldn't have to work and would have tons of money. Making sure Hester didn't see him, Richard left before she staggered out into the street.

The next afternoon, Richard knocked on Hester's door and was met by a very sleepy lady clutching a grubby dressing gown around her. When he told her he was looking into her relationship with the girls, she ushered him into a grubby hallway and slammed the front door shut. The smell in the hall nearly made him gag and the kitchen was no better. The room was filthy, with dirty dishes stacked in the sink and dishes with food stuck on them covered the grubby table. Empty gin bottles were stacked near the door and cockroaches scuttled across the floor.

Using her arm to sweep dishes from one end of the table, Hester told Richard to sit down and tell her how soon she would have the girls to stay. He told her he needed more information, which didn't please her, but eventually she sat down and answered his questions.

It turned out she was the widow of the twins' paternal great uncle's stepson—hence, the same surname—but not a blood relation. She was looking forward to her young relations doing all the household duties for their board and keep. She didn't seem to care when Richard told her the twins were only eight, but she became very agitated when he told her that Sally was blind. No way was she taking in a blind child. If she was forced to, she threatened she would leave her out on the street near the river to fend for herself.

Richard hadn't shown how shocked he was at this statement, so she then confided that some of her clients who preferred young girls would pay her a lot of money for the girl she took in. Trying hard to hide his disgust, Richard had excused himself soon after this statement, telling Hester he had to send in his report before there could be further progress. On his way home, he called in at the local police station to tell them of Hester's admission she had 'clients', some of them interested in young girls.

He later heard the police had placed a watch on her apartment the next day and had entered the apartment ten minutes after a man was ushered through the front door, to find him in bed with Hester in the front parlour. Much to Hester's fury, he admitted that he had paid for her services and worse still, the Police recognised a stolen necklace she was wearing. A thorough search of the upstairs rooms of the apartment turned up quite a stash of jewellery that linked Hester to several recent burglaries, and she was arrested on the spot.

Mary was horrified to hear this story, terrified the twins might be forced to live with this woman. Mr Lyons assured her there was little chance that would occur on such a distant and tenuous relationship, and even less chance when she was in custody and likely to be so for some time to come. However, he and Richard were going to go straight to a Magistrate in Lewes to discuss the case and hopefully get an injunction on Hester's claim and have Mary granted guardianship of the twins.

While awaiting the outcome of this meeting, Mary didn't mention anything to the girls, though she did ask Meg if she would be interested in a permanent position at Longmire Hall if the girls could stay. Meg thought this would be wonderful and, like Mary, could barely conceal her impatience while waiting for the outcome of the meeting to be revealed.

Luckily, they only had to wait a couple of days before Mary was asked to attend a meeting with the Magistrate to sign the paperwork to become the the twins' legal guardian for the period no close blood relation deemed suitable to care for young girls could be found.

Immediately on her return to Longmire Hall, Mary told the girls the news and informed them that Longmire Hall was their home for as long as they wished. She also told Meg she was now a permanent member of her staff to help look after Sally. Like the two girls, Meg was thrilled with the news and asked if she could have a few days to go back to London to hand in her notice at the hotel, and collect the remainder of her possessions in storage there. Mary told her to take as long as she needed and gave her the money for return tickets on the train, plus some money to cover her accommodation while in the city.

At first, Sally was upset at the thought of not having Meg with her but soon found there was always someone nearby keeping an eye on her or helping when she required assistance.

CHAPTER 29

While Meg was away, Robert informed Mary he had found some well-bred ponies for sale, so she joined him on a trip to the other side of Lewes to see if there were any she felt would be suitable for the boys. She was now wondering should she purchase one for Jane as well.

On arrival at their destination, they were shown a group of ten Shetland ponies in a yard beside some imposing stables that housed a number of racehorses. Mary asked the foreman if she could go into the yard with the ponies where she slowly walked amongst them, and then stood near the fence talking quietly to them. One by one, each of the ponies walked up to Mary and Robert would swear they were conversing with Mary. The foreman obviously thought the same thing as he stood there watching and shaking his head.

When Mary left the yard, three ponies followed her to the gate and the foreman stammered that they were the three he would have chosen as the best of the group for children to learn to ride on. Mary just smiled and asked if the ponies could be delivered to Longmire Hall as soon as possible.

Mary had decided to give the boys their ponies as early Christmas presents if the right ponies were available. Both Robert and James were happy to teach the children to ride and look after their ponies, and now it seemed Jane would be joining the lessons as well. The plan was for the children to ride to school when it was felt they were competent riders. This left Mary with the issue of what to give Sally as she didn't feel a pony would be advisable for her at this stage.

The next morning, Mary took Sally to the stables and introduced her to Gem. Holding Sally's hand towards Gem, Mary spoke quietly to the horse that stretched her head out to allow Sally to touch her hose. Mary encouraged Sally to rub Gem's forehead and between her ears, and then Gem gave a soft nicker and blew warm air down Sally's neck. When the startled girl heard Mary laugh, she relaxed and allowed Gem to tickle her neck with her soft lips.

Following the introduction, Mary saddled Gem then placed a pad across the saddle for a well rugged up Sally to sit on, before she swung up onto the saddle and walked the horse out of the courtyard. Allowing Gem to walk for a time to get used to Sally's extra weight, Mary told Sally they were going to visit her friend Tess at the Home Farm. She also explained that they were going to go faster but she would hold Sally tightly all the way.

As Gem began to trot, Mary felt Sally tense, but when the filly began to canter, she relaxed and began to rock to the horse's gait. By the time they reached the Home Farm gate, she was saying what fun she was having and would rather keep going, but Gem was already walking through the gate Tess had opened for them.

While Mary swung Sally down into Tess's outstretched arms, she was watching Scruffy—who had accompanied them to the farm—going through his usual routine with the farm dogs, and noticed a young dog with a yellow, curly coat creep out from under a cart and run to the back door while the other dogs were preoccupied with Scruffy.

Tess was watching the dog too and sighed, saying she didn't know what she was going to do with him. He had turned up in the yard one morning a few weeks ago, and spent most of his time hiding from the farm dogs. Tess said she hadn't the heart to get rid of him, but he was constantly being set upon by the other dogs when they caught sight of him. While Tess was explaining about the dog, he crept in behind them as they entered the kitchen.

Sally sat at the table and was happy to drink a glass of milk and listen to Mary and Tess chatting, but after a while she sensed that she was being watched. When she asked Mary who was staring at her, they realised the dog was staring at Sally with his head tilted to the side. Mary told her it was a very sad, lonely, dog that was hoping she would give him a pat and suggested she put her hand down for him to lick.

When Sally put her hand down, the dog crawled over to her and thrust his muzzle into her hand.

As she bent over to pat him, he leant up against her leg and placed his head on her lap, staring at her face. With a sigh, he shut his eyes and stayed with his head on Sally's lap until Tess asked Sally if she would like to help collect the eggs.

Tess and Mary were astounded to see the dog position himself beside Sally when she stood up, and then walk to the door with the young girl's hand resting on his back. With Tess leading the way, the dog followed, edging Sally away from puddles and walking at a pace suitable for the girl's short legs.

Mary walked behind, explaining to Sally where they were walking, telling her she was ready to assist if needed, but with every step, Sally appeared to gain more confidence in her new guide and was walking quite naturally by the time the dog stopped beside Tess at the chook yard gate.

Both women stared at one other in amazement as the dog picked up the basket Tess had put on the ground when she opened the gate. As she held Sally's hand to lead her into the chook yard, the dog walked beside Sally, totally ignoring the chooks. Tess handed the warm eggs to Sally who gently placed them in the basket still hanging from the dog's jaws.

Sally patted a couple of chooks Mary held for her, but she was more interested in walking back to the kitchen with her new friend. When he let Tess take the basket from his mouth, Sally hugged him and told him what a wonderful dog he was. The grin on his face went from ear to ear and his tail thumped a tattoo on the floor.

The next hour was spent in the kitchen, where Mary helped Tess make bread, and Sally and the dog curled up together on the mat in front of the stove. Both women were still finding it hard to believe what they had just witnessed and discussed it quietly as they kneaded the dough. Mary knew animals could sense someone in need, but had never witnessed it happen so quickly.

They both wondered if the dog could be trained to really help Sally, or whether what they had seen was just been a once-off occurrence. There was no doubt the young girl and lonely dog had struck up an instant rapport, and Tess asked Mary if she would allow Sally have the dog as a pet at the Hall.

As Tess agreed to give it a try, Mary was thinking this could solve her problem of what to give Sally when the ponies arrived for the other children, as well as possibly helping the blind girl become a little more independent. Sally was ecstatic when she was asked if she would like to take the dog home. Mary stressed it was for a trial period, but she and Tess both knew he had found a new home.

The issue of getting him to his new home was solved when Bob came in for lunch and said he would take Sally and the dog home in the cart after lunch. Mary rode home with Scruffy, wondering how he would accept the new dog.

While having lunch with some of the staff, Mary warned them of the new arrival and explained what had occurred at the farm. The twins set off after their meal to find suitable bedding and bowls while Mrs Smith told Mary she had heard of a man who had a dog trained to take him to the shops in his village in Wales.

When the cart arrived, Bob lifted Sally down and the dog jumped down and stood beside her, looking around at the people in the courtyard. Bob told Mary that initially, the dog wouldn't let him lift Sally onto the cart until she held his hand to let the dog sniff it and she told him Bob was her friend. With this in mind, she asked Sally to introduce each member of staff as they came over and watched the dog look at each person, then wag his tail.

The last introduction was to Scruffy who Mary led over after speaking quietly in his ear. Mary asked Sally to give Scruffy a hug, then to hug her dog. Surprisingly, the dog sniffed Scruffy's nose, and then walked straight back to stand beside Sally.

Asked had she named her dog, Sally said he was called Mac. As her name was Sally Martin, he would be Mac Martin! When Mary turned to walk back to the kitchen, Mac walked under Sally's hand and followed Mary, with the awestruck staff staring at Sally walking confidently beside him.

Mary was a little concerned that Mac was showing signs of overprotectiveness towards Sally and wondered how he would act when Alfie, Jack, and particularly Jane, arrived home from school. She decided to walk to the village to meet the children at the school to tell them about Mac, and asked them not to make a fuss of him and to let Sally introduce him to them.

Intrigued, the children rushed into the kitchen to see Sally cuddling a yellow dog. He looked at Jane with his head tilted, then at Sally who was smiling. Slowly he walked over to Jane, sniffed her hand then to everyone's surprise, gently took her hand in his mouth and walked back with her to stand beside Sally. He allowed Jane to stroke his head, and then he walked back to the two boys, wagging his tail and stood beside them to let them pat him.

Not a word had been said, yet the perceptive dog had understood the children were Sally's friends, especially Jane, and were to be accepted as no threat to his new friend. He lay between the two girls with his head on his paws as they excitedly swapped stories of their days activities.

When they had finished their after school snack, Sally was keen to show off Mac's ability to help her walk by herself. Arm in arm with Jane, with her other hand on Mac's back, the four children walked out into the courtyard. There Sally let go of Jane's arm and they all walked to the stables, then out into the parkland. Mary was pleased to see they all kept pace with Sally and Mac, obviously pleased she could be with them.

When the girls were in bed, with Mac on his bed on the floor beside their bed, Mary read them a story and then asked Sally not to try to walk downstairs with Mac or to leave the house by herself until Mary felt it would be safe to do so. She kissed the girls goodnight and then bent down to pat Mac who sat up and gave her a big lick on the cheek. She ruffled his ears and then whispered how pleased she was with him.

CHAPTER 30

The next morning, while Jane and Sally were dressing, Mary took Mac and Scruffy outside and was pleased to see them scamper around together until they followed her back inside. As soon as he finished his food, Mac went to sit beside Sally while she ate her breakfast.

As it was Saturday, the children spent the morning wandering around the Estate, taking Jane to areas she previously hadn't been to. Mary went with them to the lake to keep an eye on all four youngsters and was interested to watch Mac gently edging Sally away from the water's edge. Sally loved the various bird calls she could hear and asked Mary to describe the different birds to her.

Just after lunch, a covered wagon trundled into the courtyard and stopped near the stables. The curious children watched as Robert, James and the driver unloaded three small ponies and led them to the yard next to the building. Mary took the children over to the yard and told them the ponies were for Alfie, Jack and Jane to look after and learn to ride.

Quite amicably, it was decided Jane would have the bay, and Alfie would have the slightly taller pony with the white socks. Jack was thrilled to have the one he immediately called Star. Needless to say, the three children spent the rest of the afternoon out in the yard with the very patient ponies being subjected to much brushing and patting.

Mary had earlier told Sally about the ponies, explaining she had Mac and the other children would have their ponies to ride to school. Sworn to secrecy, Sally was just as excited as the others when the ponies arrived. Sally and Mac slipped away with Mary for a walk around the lake. Scruffy was happy to keep them company as the other children's attention was solely on their ponies.

On Sunday, Sally proudly walked with the others to Church and following Mary's brief discussion with the Vicar, Mac followed Mary to the front pew and lay at Sally's feet for the duration of the service. The villagers were asked not to pat Mac while he led Sally through the Church yard, but all were smiling as the dog and girl walked past them.

All the staff were thrilled to see the little girl looking so happy, and were careful to keep an eye on her and her dog as they found their way around the house and the yard.

The boys and Jane had their first riding lessons after dinner with Robert, James, and Mary leading them around the yard, initially just walking, then bumping along at the trot. At the end of the lesson, they brushed and fed their ponies and then raced inside to excitedly tell everyone they met about their new skills.

The next morning, after the ponies had been fed, James took the children to school, with Sally and Mac sitting beside him. Villagers they met called out good morning to Sally and when James told who had called out, Sally politely used their name when she replied.

When Meg returned two days later, and James drove the cart around the corner of the Hall, she was amazed to see Sally walking alone with a dog in the courtyard. She noted that as soon as the cart came into view, the dog moved Sally to a safe place near the stable, and the girl moved confidently wherever the dog led her.

Sally couldn't contain her delight at Meg's return, and Mac quickly picked up on her excitement. He sat quietly watching their reunion for a while, and then gave a gentle woof as though reminding Sally to introduce him. This done, he looked at Meg with her arm around Sally's shoulder, wagged his tail then walked in front of them into the house.

At first, Sally was upset, thinking he had run away until Meg explained he was sharing her with Meg. She also explained there would still be times when Sally would need people helping her and that Mac would need some time off. Happy with this, Sally hugged Meg and walked inside with her.

After watching the dog and child together during the day, Meg and Mary sat together after dinner to discuss how best to progress the dog's training. He seemed to instinctively know how to guide her, but how could they teach him where to go when Sally couldn't see to tell him?

CHAPTER 31

The next morning, just after James left to take the children to school, a lone horseman rode down the drive, astride a magnificent black horse. Opening the front door, Mary was delighted to see that the rider was Hugh Watson. As he dismounted, she ran down the steps to greet him, Scruffy close behind her. He ran straight up to Hugh and licked the hand held out to him, then walked beside him as Hugh and Mary walked around to the courtyard where Robert took the horse into the stables.

Delighted to see Hugh again, Mary led him into the Hall where he admitted he was starving, having not had breakfast before leaving Lewes. Mary took him to the breakfast room and asked Polly to have Mrs Smith prepare a hot breakfast for her visitor. While waiting for the food to be brought in, Mary asked how he had managed to arrive earlier than planned.

He explained that following their graduation, all students had a final interview with the Master of the College to discuss future employment. When Hugh mentioned he had been offered the role of Estate Supervisor at Longmire Estate when he left the College, the Master immediately released him from further duties and wished him luck with his new job.

Not only that, one of the staff members who came from near Lewes arranged for him to stay the night with his family, who had a horse stud just the other side of the town. While there, he saw the black mare and decided to buy her, rather than hiring a horse in Lewes.

Unfortunately, not long after passing through Lewes, the mare had cast a shoe so he had to return to town to have new shoes fitted. By the time he was ready to leave for Longmire Hall, it was too late in the afternoon to ride alone in the dark on an unknown road. He had stabled his horse for the night and stayed in a hotel, leaving for Longmire Hall that morning at dawn.

While Hugh ate, Mary asked Polly to have a room prepared for Hugh, then poured herself another cup of coffee and explained about the new additions to the household since her arrival home. When Hugh was ready, Mary showed him to his room and left him to freshen up after his ride, telling him she would wait for him downstairs.

In his room, Hugh was feeling rather uneasy, as having seen the stately residence Mary called home and the servants calling her 'm'lady', the realisation that she really was a Countess hit home.

While she had been at Oakdale it just hadn't seemed real and had been easy to ignore when they were just two young people together. He had been looking forward to seeing her again, as he had become very fond of her and had missed her terribly since they parted company in London.

When he met her downstairs, Mary sensed he was feeling unsure of himself and tried to dispel his concerns, telling him she was still the same person, despite the grand setting. She introduced him to the indoor staff as the new Estate Supervisor, then took him out to the stables where he met Robert again and James, who had just returned with Sally and Mac.

When Sally was lifted to the ground, Hugh was amused to see the yellow dog jump down and stand beside her, watching him warily until Mary introduced him to Hugh. Then he relaxed and waited while Mary introduced Sally and Hugh.

When Meg appeared at the back door and called to Sally, Hugh stood in amazement as he watched the young girl place her hand on Mac's back and walk confidently with him straight to Meg and through the back door. Like everyone else, Hugh found it hard to believe that Sally and Mac had only been together a week and that Mac had been a lost, terrified dog before they met.

Breakfast the next morning was a new experience for Hugh, with all the staff, plus four children and Mary, all chatting away, with no hint of the subservience he understood most of the aristocracy commanded of their servants. Their one obvious concession to Mary's title was to call her 'm'lady'.

When it was time for school, Hugh watched Mac guide Sally out to the cart and wait to be lifted onto the seat after James had lifted Sally up.

Meg told Mary she would like to spend time with Sally, teaching her how to use her cane while walking with Mac and also to show her a book with raised letters she had bought while in London. This suited Mary well as she intended to take Hugh around the three farms to meet the farmers he would be working with as the Estate manager.

When they saddled up their horses, Mary and Hugh visited the Home Farm first where Mary introduced Hugh to Bob, Tess, and Will. The men were just about to move cows to the upper pasture so Hugh went with them while Mary helped Tess separate the cream, ready to make butter. On his return to the house, Hugh happily took the skim milk out to tip in the trough in the pigsty.

After a quick cup of tea, Mary and Hugh rode up to Glendale to introduce Hugh to Thomas and Paul. Initially a little hesitant to talk, the men soon relaxed as Hugh chatted about their sheep and the work they did up in the hills, all the while fondling their two dogs who normally didn't like strangers.

On the way to Old Joe's farm, as it was still called, Mary took Hugh up to the Lookout, a high hill overlooking a lot of the Estate, where they stopped to eat the lunch packed by Mrs Smith. They didn't linger too long, as despite the weak sunshine, there was a cold breeze and Mary was learning the afternoons were getting quite short at this stage of the year in England.

Matthew and John were keen to chat to Hugh and Mary, explaining the changes they had made since Old Joe left. John in particular, wanted to talk to Hugh about the Royal Agricultural College where Hugh had been studying.

Hugh had a lot to think about on their ride home and was happy to go up to his room for a long, hot bath before changing for dinner. He was excited at the prospect of becoming the Estate Supervisor but also a little nervous about taking on the job.

Apart from collecting rents and being responsible for maintenance of Estate infrastructure and machinery, he was also going to be asked to work initially with the Estate farmers to help them modernise their enterprises where possible, improving their pastures and stock breeding.

As pasture/crop management and animal breeding were his strongest areas of interest, he felt he could help the farmers make their businesses more profitable. When established, he was also going to be asked to help neighbouring farmers who were interested in what he had to offer.

After dinner that evening, Mary and Hugh retired to the study where she showed him the Estate accounts ledgers, as well as the rent books. She told him about Mr Morris and his demise, plus what she had done since then. Hugh was impressed that she had undertaken the job herself until a suitable replacement was found, not only because she was a Peer of the Realm but also because she was a woman. Although he was beginning to realise she was no ordinary woman and didn't think it would be wise to comment on what he had been brought up to think a woman's role should be.

As the next day was fine, after a quick look at the Estate office, Mary, Hugh, Sally, Mac and Scruffy walked to the village. Meg said she would like to stay home to prepare some lessons for Sally. Scruffy, as usual, dashed all over the place but Hugh was impressed to see that no matter what Scruffy was doing, Mac totally ignored him and concentrated on guiding Sally away from puddles and rough areas of the road.

In order to save Sally from becoming too tired, Hugh offered to give her a piggyback ride. When Mac was satisfied she didn't need him, he raced off to join Scruffy, snuffling around in the hedgerow along the side of the road. Earlier in the morning, Hugh had checked Mac's teeth and said he was about twelve months old, a little older than Scruffy. To watch them scampering along the road, it was easy to see they were still basically pups, one with a grey, shaggy coat and long legs, and the other lower to the ground with a yellow, curly coat.

On arrival at the village, Mary took Hugh into all the shops, the pub, and other business premises, plus the vicarage to meet many of the villagers. She also introduced him to the many people who stopped to chat to her as they walked along the street. Hugh had never been in a village where a member of the gentry was genuinely recognised as a friend.

While walking back to the Hall, watching Hugh piggybacking Sally again, Mary decided it would be a good idea to buy one of the new Governess Carts she had seen advertised in a rural paper. Meg could use it when taking Sally around the Estate. It would also be handy for taking the other children to and from school, freeing up James and the cart.

Hugh had informed her before breakfast that he was happy to take on the Estate Supervisor position, so she told him his first job was to purchase a Governess Cart and suitable pony as soon as possible. As he had carried Sally nearly all the way back to the Hall, he thought this was a jolly good idea.

CHAPTER 32

Three days after his arrival at the Estate, Hugh attended his first Rent day. Mr Lyons and Mary sat in the Office with him as each tenant entered to pay their rent. Anyone Hugh hadn't already met was encouraged to tell him where they lived, and who they worked for, as well as their family status.

Despite the cold weather, most people were quite cheerful, lingering to chat and to sample Mrs Smith's lamb shank and vegetable soup and hot bread rolls, both supplied in copious amounts throughout the day. Both boys and Jane were given the day off school; Jack to help chop up the vegetables that Alfie regularly brought into the kitchen.

Jane helped the twins wash the pots, while to the amazement of people who hadn't met them before, Sally and Mac both carried out baskets full of the hot bread rolls and took the empty ones back to the kitchen to be refilled.

Following Rent day, Mary showed Hugh through the cottage Mr Morris had occupied, explaining it was available rent-free as part of his remuneration as Farm Manager. He could choose to have meals with the other staff in the Hall, or cook his own from provisions supplied from the kitchen. Hugh said he was keen to move into his own home, though he would enjoy the communal meals in the Hall when he was on the estate.

Mary had also discussed with Meg the possibility of her moving to the second cottage with Jane and Sally (and Mac of course). Meg thought this would be a great idea to give the girls the sense of having something more akin to a family home.

She wondered if the boys might like to join them but when asked, the boys were adamant that they were happy in their room in the Hall and didn't want to move. Both Archie and Jack adored Mary and to them the Hall was their home. The large bedroom next to Mary's was theirs to retreat to whenever they wished to, which gave them both a great sense of security. They had their own bathroom and plenty of room for the toys and games they had accumulated. Provided they kept the room tidy, Jane cleaned it and set the fire but the boys made their own bed and carried up the coal for their fire. Scruffy slept in their room too, and they were sure he would prefer to stay put as well.

As Mary's official duties increased, she had to travel to Lewes more often. She felt she was beginning to impose on the Lyons' hospitality too much, so she asked Mr Lyons to look for a suitable house for her to buy.

A week later, he showed Mary through a thatched cottage with a lovely rose garden at the front and large back garden, with a vegetable garden, small orchard, and a double stable with attached Grooms quarters, with access to the rear lane. The cottage had a large kitchen and scullery, a dining and living room on the ground floor, and four bedrooms, one with a maid's room, a bathroom with running water, and an indoor water closet upstairs. Mary loved the cottage and decided it would be best to have someone living in it; otherwise, it would be empty for more days than she would be staying.

Celia introduced her to a young, recently widowed lady with two small children, whose husband had recently drowned when his fishing boat sank. She had been turned out of her house and was desperately looking for accommodation for herself and her children.

Mary arranged for Gwen and her two children to move into the cottage as soon as the paperwork was signed. They had use of two of the bedrooms while the third bedroom with the maids room, was to be kept in readiness for Mary to stay in whenever in Lewes and the fourth as a spare bedroom.

Hugh quickly settled into his new job, riding out to the three farms early in the morning, often staying all day helping with whatever jobs needed doing. Some nights he arrived back quite late and was very thankful for the meal Mrs Smith would leave in his kitchen. The farmers were pleased to see Hugh and were ready to listen when he discussed ways that might be more profitable, as well as make their job a bit easier.

Late in the first week of December, he visited the Grey brothers at Glendale, to find Thomas' house bound with a badly swollen knee, the result of slipping on ice in the yard the previous night. Both men were very concerned that Paul would be unable to carry out all the work required before it snowed on the higher land. Hugh asked Paul to ride down to the hall to tell Lady Mary he would stay at Glendale for a few days and to ask her to pack him some extra warm clothes.

Mary returned with Paul, both horses carrying packed saddlebags. Mary checked Thomas's knee and told him he should stay inside and keep his leg up as much as possible. Hugh fashioned a crutch from a small limb, then sent Mary on her way home so she would be riding in daylight.

The days were getting shorter and once again, Mary was having trouble dealing with the opposite seasons, especially as Christmas was rapidly approaching and there had been a couple of snow falls already—a far cry from the scorching heat, with the constant threat of bushfires of her previous Christmases in Australia.

Having never seen snow before, Mary was as excited as the children when out making snowmen and throwing snowballs. She did, however, quickly realise that despite its beauty, it made life much harder for the farmers and outside staff.

There were plans to have a Christmas party in the Hall for the villagers in the week prior to Christmas Day, plus a 'family' Christmas dinner for all the residents of the Hall, plus invited guests. While looking forward to the planned Christmas festivities, Mary was painfully aware it would be the first anniversary of her mother's death just after Christmas. Also, she was missing Aunt Clara and Graham, her family members so far away.

Awoken by thunder early one dark, stormy, December morning, Mary lay thinking of the dramatic changes that had occurred since that fateful day, nearly twelve months ago when her mother had died. At that time, she was an unpaid worker on the family dairy farm in Australia, and had since travelled to the other side of the world, and was now a Peer of the Realm, an extremely wealthy young lady, living in a huge stately mansion, with staff and four young children dependant on her.

Thinking of all the amazing things that had happened since she had arrived in England eight months ago, Mary wondered what the coming New Year could possibly have in store for her.

Printed in the United States
By Bookmasters